THE PLUS ONE RESCUE

TEXAS HOTLINE SERIES, BOOK #1

JO GRAFFORD

Copyright © 2020 by Jo Grafford.

Second Edition. This book was previously part of the Disaster City Search and Rescue Series. It has since been revised and recovered to launch the Texas Hotline Series.

Cover Design by Jo Grafford.

All rights reserved.

No part of this book may be reproduced in any form without written permission from the author or publisher, except as permitted by U.S. copyright law.

ISBN: 978-1-944794-57-6

GET A FREE BOOK!

Join my mailing list to be the first to know about new releases, freebies, special discounts, and Bonus Content. Plus, you get a FREE sweet romance book for signing up!

https://BookHip.com/JNNHTK

ACKNOWLEDGMENTS

Thank you so much to my wonderful beta readers — Mahasani and J. Sherlock. I also want to thank my completely amazing editor, Cathleen Weaver. Lastly, I want to give a shout-out to my Cuppa Jo Readers on Facebook for reading and loving my books!

ABOUT THIS SERIES

Welcome to the Texas Hotline, a team of search and rescue experts — police officers, firefighters, expert divers, and more. In an emergency, your sweet and swoon-worthy rescuer is only a phone call away.

CHAPTER 1: COMING HOME
AXEL

Why me? Why did I get to come home?

Not too long ago, Axel Hammerstone had been a penniless kid in foster care — no family, no roots. During his stint in the Marines, he'd met men and women who were far wealthier, far more educated, and far better connected. But none of those things had increased their chances of survival. That was the irony of war.

There would be no welcome home posters when he landed. No one to cry happy tears. Not that he wanted anyone to cry over him. It had been a physically and mentally exhausting trip, one that had taken months if he counted his stopover in the hospital.

Though his plane was only minutes from landing in Dallas, he couldn't have felt less like celebrating. He stared out the window of the Boeing

747 as it circled the Dallas/Fort Worth International Airport. It was overcast with a hint of rain. Decently windy, if the air currents rocking the wings of the plane were any indication. *Kind of poetic, actually.* It was as if the sky had decided to weep a few tears for him since there was no one else to.

He'd spent nine months in the craggy wilderness of Afghanistan, followed by another six months of convalescing at a specialized burn unit in San Antonio, followed by yet a few more weeks of medical out-processing at Fort Sam Houston. And now that it was over, there was no one coming to so much as greet him at the airport. No wife or children. Not even a girlfriend. He had no ties to anyone, actually. His foster parents — who hadn't sent a single letter or care package during his entire deployment overseas — had already texted to let him know they were tied up at some court hearing.

Axel had briefly considered notifying the family of his best friend that he was returning home. The Zanes probably would have met him at the airport if he had, but he saw no point in adding the sight of him to their overwhelming grief.

He and their only son, Marcus Zane, had played football together in high school, graduated together, and enlisted in the Marines together. Fifteen months ago, they'd also been deployed to Kandahar together. Axel made the sign of the cross on his chest. *Rest in peace, brother.* Unfortunately, Marcus wasn't one of the lucky ones. He should have been, but he wasn't.

The plane landed with a bumbling double bounce that made the elderly woman sitting to his right gasp and grab hold of the armrests with both heavily be-ringed hands. Her skin was so pale that it made her painted fingernails look like they were dripping blood. They hadn't exchanged two words the entire hour of their flight, which was fine with him. He wasn't in the mood for chatting. However, he noted that she seemed to be having difficulty catching her breath. It was something a man trained to serve and protect was unable to ignore.

He bent his head a fraction to get a better look at her face. "Are you alright, ma'am?"

Her slightly upturned brown eyes were wide with fear. The crinkles at the corners of her eyes were like dozens of tiny paper folds. She blinked a few times and slowly raised her face to his. "Did we crash?"

The ludicrous question amused him, but he kept a straight face. "Nah. We just landed with a bit of a bounce. Pilot probably needs a refill on his coffee." They were flying first class, thanks to the automatic upgrade he'd been given when he flashed his military ID at the ticket counter, so he glanced around for the nearest stewardess. He wondered what the odds were of securing a bottle of water this late in the trip.

His travel companion sure looked like she could use some refreshment.

Her tight lips relaxed into a hint of a smile. "For a second there, you sounded just like my Kento." She looked like a typical first-class traveler in her black designer pants suit, lacy white blouse, and fat diamond pendant necklace. Her manicure was perfect, as was her makeup. Every silver hair in her French braided up-do was in place. She was clearly of Asian descent.

Axel raised his eyebrows at her. "And he is?"

"The love of my life." She released her white-knuckled grip on the armrests to sit up more fully in her seat.

He felt a pang of something. Envy? Resentment? *Wow! That's just great. I'm jealous of an old lady.* He scrubbed a hand over his jaw, feeling like his life had just hit a new low. He forced himself to swallow the prickle of bitterness on his tongue. "Guess that means your cowboy will be waiting for you outside the jet ramp." *Lucky you!*

This time, she chuckled as she spared him another sideways glance. "I'm actually returning home after paying him a visit. My granddaughter is the one who will be waiting for me."

"Uh, that's nice." Axel sensed a story, but didn't consider it his place to ask questions.

"It is. She puts up a terrible fuss every time I

make my annual visit to the Sam Houston National Cemetery."

Ah. Axel's brain froze. Her husband was gone. Just like Marcus was gone, along with way too many of his other Marine buddies. His mind drifted back to that fateful night on the outskirts of Kandahar.

"SO I MET this girl the other night." Marcus nudged Axel with one broad shoulder as they jostled along a dirt road in their armored light utility vehicle. They were standing in the turret opening. Axel was serving as their primary lookout, while Marcus manned their mounted .50 caliber machine gun.

"Right." Axel didn't bother muffling a snort. They were deployed, for crying out loud. They had no social life. None whatsoever. Other than the handful of female Marines in their unit and the one female at the last MP checkpoint, there were no women in their lives.

"You talking about the one who frisked us at the MP checkpoint?" Axel shook his head in exasperation. She was attractive in a blonde, beach-babe sort of way. He'd give Marcus that. But she hadn't seemed very interested in their sandy, sweaty platoon. At least not in the romantic way. All she'd done was process them and their equipment through the checkpoint and provide an intelligence update about the pack of terrorists they were tracking through the surrounding foothills.

Marcus grinned and flexed his upper arms. "What can I say? She liked what she saw."

Axel used his shoulder to shove his friend back. "Gee! What gave it away? Her snarl when you asked for her number?" Marcus was such a player. Ever since their high school football days, he'd been landing dates with the prettiest, most popular girls — from their homecoming queen to the winner of their town beauty pageant. Normally, the guy could charm the skin off a rattlesnake, but the gorgeous military police chick at their last checkpoint had appeared solidly immune to his attempts at flirting with her.

Marcus waggled his black brows, making a trio of wrinkles form in the center of his wide, dark forehead. He pushed his Kevlar lower, like one might do to a favorite Stetson, hiding his expression. "That and the fact that she whispered her cell phone number to me when she handed back my ID."

"You're kidding!" Axel shook his head at his friend, whose brows remained raised in challenge. "Okay. You're not kidding. Wow! Well, there you go, man, living up to your reputation." He hardly saw the point in flirting with a soldier they'd likely never see again. A thought struck him. "You do realize it's probably an old number." One that wouldn't work when they got back to the States. Most soldiers he knew cancelled their cell phone plans while they were overseas. It saved them a decent chunk of cash.

"Oh, ye of little faith!" Marcus ducked his head and lowered his voice, so it wouldn't carry down to their driver. "She promised me it'll work when she pops her sim card back in."

Axel shook his head again. "It'll be another three months, at least, before we get out of here." None of their personal electronic devices would work until they were back in U.S. air space.

"So? All I gotta do is remember her number for that long."

"What makes you think she'll even remember you when you call?" *Much less pick up when the phone rings?* Axel couldn't believe they were having such a mundane conversation about girls and dating on the outskirts of Kandahar. Their days of wearing blue jeans and drinking soda seemed so far away here in the craggy foothills of the Sulaiman Range. Fingers of green vegetation streaked down the dusty mountain ridges, though the distant peaks of the Hindu Kush remained capped with white. It was early March, the in-between season in terms of temperature and precipitation.

"Because she's the one."

Um, okay. "If you say so." Axel wasn't buying it. He didn't believe in things like love at first sight. A blur of movement on the other side of the mountain pass captured his attention. Their trio of armored utility vehicles was escorting a much larger Marine convoy through the pass. They were the forward-most eyes and ears.

"I do." Marcus cocked his gloved thumb and forefinger like a hand gun.

"Sounds like you're already practicing your wedding vows," Axel scoffed, whipping out his binoculars for a closer look.

"Practice makes perfect." Marcus leaned closer to his scope to follow Axel's line of sight.

A flash of sun hitting glass against the distant mountain ridge was Axel's only warning there was trouble ahead. A sniper, most likely. He slapped his hand on the side of the vehicle to get their driver's attention. "Puppies and kittens about two clicks north," he growled into his shoulder microphone. It was a private joke — his platoon's way of identifying enemy combatants.

The driver immediately halted their vehicle.

"Got 'em marked." Marcus rattled off the coordinates, and Axel swiftly radioed them in. "Two tangos for sure. Maybe three."

Three snipers. Axel's pulse sped in anticipation of the coming encounter. A burst of adrenaline in times like these was good. He always welcomed the way it heightened his senses and helped him focus.

The rogues in the mountains were, if anything, unpredictable in their construction of hodgepodge fortifications. Most times, they were holed up with nothing more than a handful of M-16s. Once in a while, however, they managed to score a grenade launcher, which meant Axel and his comrades always needed to expect the unexpected.

"Another tango spotted," the lookout in the vehicle directly behind them warned. "Click and a half east."

"Tango spotted south. We're boxed in," the last lookout chimed in breathlessly.

Okay. It was starting to sound like a whole lot of not good. Axel's blood pounded through his veins as he bent over his sniper rifle, took aim, and awaited his captain's orders.

"Charlie mike with extreme prejudice!" Captain Ramos barked across the line. It was a direct order to continue their mission, which was simple — to eradicate the countryside of enemy combatants seeking to unseat the newly installed government.

Axel forced himself to breathe in and out in an even cadence. He would need all his wits about him if they were rolling their way into a bonafide terrorist stronghold. At the very least, his day was about to get a lot more interesting.

"I'll be expecting you to rent a tux when we get home, bro," Marcus tightened his finger on the butterfly trigger of his .50 cal.

If their situation had been any less serious, Axel would've laughed. His friend was referring, of course, to their longstanding promise to serve as best man at each other's weddings. "Don't you need to propose to her first?"

"A mere technicality." In the next second, his .50 caliber machine gun was belching lead and smoke.

A much larger-than-expected explosion billowed in the distance. Then a series of subsequent explosions worked their way in a half-circle around their trio of armored vehicles.

"What the—?" Marcus lifted his head from his scope.

"It's like we triggered some sort of chain reaction." Axel watched in growing alarm as the explosions circled ever closer to their vehicle. "We have to get out of here." *Or be roasted alive.*

Unfortunately, there was no driving their way out of this. He hastily scanned the terrain. The northern and southern routes were in flames. The east ended in a fairly steep drop-off, leaving their only way of escape to the west. *Sort of.* It was all mountains — the kind that went straight up. But he and his comrades were fresh out of options, since it was the only route that wasn't on fire. Or wouldn't plunge them straight to Kingdom Come.

Trails of fire shot across the path of their vehicle, enveloping them in smoke and making it harder to breathe. Axel instinctively slid his black fabric neck warmer over his mouth and nose, knowing they might only have seconds left to evacuate. Once the flames reached their gas tank, it would turn their truck into a bomb.

"Out! Now!" Marcus fumbled with the bolts on his .50 cal.

"Leave it!" Axel shouted. "There's no time." He slapped Marcus's shoulder for emphasis.

His friend nodded, leaped to the ground, and turned around to assist Axel down with his sniper rifle.

"Come on!" Axel jogged away from Marcus and used his fist to pound on the driver's door. The young corporal stared back, his blue eyes dazed with disbelief. *Yeah, I get it, buddy. We never got to practice this exact scenario. Improvise and adapt!* Axel flung open the door and yanked the guy by his shirt collar from his seat. "Move!" He shoved him in the direction of the nearest mountain.

The armored truck in the middle of their convoy made a sizzling sound.

"Out! Everyone, get out!" Axel frantically waved them toward the ditch.

The occupants of the vehicle leaped and rolled from its doors only seconds before it exploded. They dove into the ditch as windows, leather seat cushions, and gun parts flew everywhere.

Something hot seared Axel's shoulder blades, knocking the wind from his chest. He silently mouthed a prayer into the dirt. His foster parents hadn't been church goers, and he'd never considered himself to be an overly religious person, but he was beginning to understand one old saying, in particular — that there were no atheists inside of fox holes.

The screams and shouts around him gave him the energy to lift his head. More veins of fire were shooting in the direction of the third vehicle. "This way!" he bellowed, reaching for the nearest thing to wave in the air. It turned out to be a length of burning canvas. He waved it back and forth like a fiery flag, ushering the remaining soldiers into the ditch with him and the others. They made it a mere fraction of a second before their vehicle exploded.

He did a hasty count after the biggest pieces of carnage settled. There were only eight men. They were missing one. His fevered brain immediately recognized who it was. *Marcus!*

Axel's head spun from side to side, taking in their surroundings. "Marcus!" he shouted, low-crawling from the ditch. Keeping his head down, he dragged himself by his elbows over scalding pieces of metal that burned their way through the sleeves of his uniform. Through the smoke, he could just barely make out the silhouette of their last vehicle standing — the one he and Marcus had ridden into the hellish mountain pass.

There was Marcus, up on the roof, struggling to loosen the bolts of his machine gun.

"What are you doing?" Unfortunately, the smoke

had rendered Axel's voice a thick, scratchy version of its former tenor. He doubted Marcus heard him.

Understanding his friend was trying to save the weapon, but fearing he'd never be able to loosen it in time, Axel dragged himself to his knees. He reached for the bumper and pulled himself to his feet. Bullets scored the ground around him. *Great.* That meant the terrorists surrounding them were alive and well, preparing to pick off any and all American survivors like ants. It was a horrifyingly well-planned ambush. No wonder Marcus was working so hard to free the .50 cal. They might need it to stay alive in the coming hours.

Mercy! Axel squinted up at the sky, wondering when the Air Force would arrive to launch their next strike. *Any time now would be nice.*

"Marcus!" He reached his friend and pounded on the side of the vehicle to get his attention.

Marcus either didn't hear him or chose to ignore him. Gritting his teeth, Axel swung himself up. More gunshots sounded. This time, his whole body jolted from the impact. He'd been hit. How many times was hard to tell, though it felt like his left leg was on fire.

Marcus's dark gaze fastened on him in horror. "Get out!" he roared.

Axel shook his head, no longer able to speak. He extended a hand. *Not without you.* If the terrorists failed to pick them off, the vehicle was about to blow up. He was surprised it had lasted this long. *Come on, brother. If you really expect me to wear that tux, we have to get out of here alive.*

More shots sounded, and Axel's other leg went numb. *Uh-oh!* He didn't dare look down.

With a roar of fury, Marcus swung the .50 cal around and opened fire in the direction of the bullets peppering their truck. Smoke billowed from beneath the hood as the flames reached them at long last.

Screaming something Axel couldn't understand, Marcus reached for Axel's arm and propelled the two of them over the side of the vehicle. Instead of heading for the ditch, however, they rolled through the dust toward the steep drop off.

The rocks and sand blurred as Axel clawed the ground and tried to slow their progress. *This is the wrong way!* "What are you—?"

They rolled over the side of the cliff in the same second that their armored truck exploded. Metal parts flew over their heads. Axel managed to grab hold of a scraggly bush. He held on, despite his fast-waning strength.

More explosions sounded — big, deep, earth-shaking ones. Much larger ones than before. They were familiar sounds, music to Axel's ears. He nearly wept with relief at the knowledge that the Air Force had finally arrived. *God bless America!* It lent him a burst of adrenaline. He used it to continue holding on, burying his face against the side of the cliff as explosion after explosion rocked both ends of the mountain pass. Debris rained down on him, but his rock solid Kevlar shielded his head from the worst of it.

Though he couldn't feel his legs any longer, he felt a heavy pressure, like the mountain itself had him in its grasp and was trying to yank him loose. It was fast weakening his grip on the bush. Glancing down, he discovered what was weighing him down. He stared into Marcus's upturned face. The only thing in the world keeping his best friend from free-falling down the side of the cliff was his grip on Axel's ankles.

"Hold on!" Axel croaked. He feverishly struggled to shift his weight, seeking any position that would free one of his hands so he could pull Marcus to safety. *If I can hook my elbow around the bush just so...*

"Don't!" Marcus shook his head in warning. Never had his dark gaze been so full of brotherly affection. Or unwavering intent. "There's no reason for us both to die today."

A chill shot through Axel's chest. *No! Whatever you're thinking, don't do it!* He frenziedly renewed his efforts to get a better grip on the bush, so he could pull them to safety.

"Semper fi." Marcus mouthed the words and let go.

Axel's mouth froze in an open-mouthed scream,

though no sound came out. Blackness billowed like storm clouds across his vision.

The last thing he remembered was hands. Lots of hands reaching over the ledge to pull him up.

But it was too late. Marcus was already gone.

The blackness took over.

"MISTER, ah…sir! Are you alright, sir?"

Axel dragged his head upward to find a stewardess standing over him. At her elbow was the fancily dressed Asian lady. Both were peering anxiously at him.

The stewardess was a killer blonde, maybe in her early thirties, with a pitying look in her eyes. "I've already put in a call for a wheelchair. I'm happy to ring for an ambulance, too, if—"

"No!"

She jumped at the vehemence in his voice.

"No," he repeated in a gentler tone. "I'm fine. Really." He pushed himself to his feet, hating how shaky his knees felt. There was no way he was letting anyone roll him through the airport in a stinking wheelchair. "I got out of the hospital recently." He forced a grin he didn't feel. "They wouldn't have let me out if I wasn't ready. Trust me." For the most part, his physical wounds were healed. The PTSD he was learning to live with.

"I'll make sure he gets to where he's going." With a toss of her regal head, the tiny Asian lady actually reached for Axel's sand-colored backpack that was resting in the overhead compartment.

Over my dead body! Muffling a chuckle, he reached up and hauled the heavy bag down, tossing it over one shoulder. He reached for her roller bag next. "I'll gladly accept your company, though. Lead the way, general."

Dark eyes twinkling, she nodded and walked ahead of him with a grace that belied her years. "I'm Aimi Kimiko, by the way. I don't believe I caught your name."

"Axel," he supplied, wondering what the point was in introducing himself to a woman he'd probably never see again. "Axel Hammerstone."

"A very soldierly name." Her smile was curious.

He glanced down at his stone-washed jeans and plain black t-shirt, wondering how in heaven's name anyone could deduce from his clothing that he was a soldier.

"Dog tags," she supplied in a loud whisper with a merry glance over her shoulder.

Oh. Right. He eyed the unmistakable rectangular outline of the tags beneath his shirt. Though he wasn't required to wear them anymore, it was turning out to be a hard habit to break after having them around his neck for the past eight years. They were all but part of his skin.

The pilot and co-pilot waited somberly in the entry way. "Thank you for your service, soldier." The pilot gave him a swift salute. His co-pilot mirrored his movements.

Apparently, Axel's travel companion wasn't the only one who'd noticed his dog tags.

"Eh, well, we all have our jobs." He shrugged. "Thanks for getting us to the ground in one piece." He felt a flush creep up his neck. He'd never been good at accepting compliments.

To his surprise, Mrs. Kimiko rounded on the pilot with a feisty expression riding her fine-boned features. "There was a little more bounce to the landing than I prefer, young man. I wasn't the only passenger praying that you have the sense to refill your coffee before the next flight." She winked at Axel.

The co-pilot burst out laughing and sent a playful punch in the direction of the pilot's shoulder, which inevitably reminded Axel of the easygoing banter he'd always shared with Marcus.

Ducking his head to block out the sight, he hurried after Mrs. Kimiko. They walked side-by-side to the baggage claim area.

"What's next for you, Mr. Hammerstone?" she inquired in a soft, musical voice.

He had no earthly idea. "Guess I'm still figuring that out."

"You will," she returned with a conviction he didn't share.

He wished he could borrow a dose of her optimism.

"Oh, there's my granddaughter!" She raised a hand and waved it excitedly. The movement made her diamond bracelet catch the sunlight and glitter like fire.

Fire. Just the thought of fire made Axel feel the scorch of Kandahar all over again.

"You should meet her." Mrs. Kimiko shot him a sly female look from beneath her dark lashes. "She's not a soldier like you, but she's certainly in the business of protecting and serving. She's a dog handler, actually."

A dog handler? Axel's brows shot up. He failed to see how training dogs had any resemblance to being a Marine.

"She trains search and rescue workers and their dogs how to save lives." She gave him a comical frown and swatted the air. "Kristi can explain it better than I can. How about I introduce the two of you?" She slowed her gait to stare hopefully up at him.

Axel shook his head in genuine regret. "Maybe some other time." As much as he appreciated the offer, he wasn't good company right now, and he sure as heck wasn't scouting around for a date. He had nothing to offer. No job. No home. No stability. He wasn't even sure where he was going to spend the night.

Mrs. Kimiko looked disappointed. "Maybe some other time, then. I'm glad our paths crossed."

"Me, too, ma'am." He relinquished the handle of her black and gray plaid suitcase and dropped back a few steps as she hurried forward to be swept into the arms of her granddaughter.

His jaw dropped. Aimi Kimiko's granddaughter was — no joke! — the most stunning woman he'd ever laid eyes on. She had long, dark hair with sassy, lighter brown highlights that draped nearly to her waist. Though she was as petite as her grandmother, she made up for her lack of height with a pair of strappy red stilettos that accentuated her sun-kissed legs. She was wearing a navy denim dress that hung just above her knees, with a silver belt circling her doll-like waist.

Even more remarkable than her beauty was the tender moment she shared with her grandmother. After several affectionate hugs, they appeared to be talking at the same time — two people who were clearly overjoyed to see each other. They shared the kind of bond that only existed between families. They belonged to each other in ways he'd never belonged to another person and probably never would.

Something twisted in his chest; for a moment, he

would have given anything to have Aimi Kimiko's granddaughter look at him that way.

I'm an idiot. That's what Marcus would've called him for passing up Ms. Kimiko's offer to introduce him to such a gorgeous, kindhearted creature. Marcus would already be halfway across the room. A few seconds from now, he'd have her phone number memorized.

But Axel wasn't Marcus. His limp felt a little more pronounced as he joined the latest flood of passengers disembarking from the security gates. First, he had a mound of baggage to collect. Then it would be time to figure out what came next — what was even supposed to come next.

He barely felt like putting one foot in front of the other, but Marcus had given his all so that Axel could keep marching. *I'll make your sacrifice count every day I have left, brother. I promise!*

CHAPTER 2: AWKWARD INTRODUCTIONS

KRISTI

All morning long, Kristi Kimiko had held on to the feeling that there was something extraordinarily special about today. For one thing, she'd been officially notified she was receiving a pay raise. For another thing, it was absolutely wonderful having her grandmother home again. *Sheesh!* That was an understatement. Kristi was so relieved the old dear had made it back to Dallas safe and sound that her knees felt wobbly with relief. Women fast approaching eighty should *not* be allowed to travel alone. Period. Unfortunately, it was an argument she'd failed to win thus far, despite five years of trying.

"I met the most wonderful young man on my flight home," her grandmother gushed.

"What? I didn't know you were on the market again," Kristi teased. She flipped a handful of hair over her shoulder and cocked her head with a look of feigned innocence.

"He was a handsome devil, too." Aimi Kimiko ignored the jibe. "A Marine. I was hoping to introduce the two of you, but—"

"But he caught wind of your ill-concealed matchmaking plans and took off running in the opposite direction, huh?" Her grandmother was shamelessly transparent in her never-ending quest to find the perfect match for her only granddaughter.

"He didn't run." Her grandmother looked mildly offended. "He limped, and it just so happened to be in the same direction we're heading." She pointed one delicate finger toward the baggage claim area, making Kristi wince at the number of diamonds glittering from her fingers and wrist. In addition to having no fear of traveling alone at her age, she apparently had no concerns about being mugged, either — something else they were going to have to discuss soon.

Kristi glanced toward the baggage area, not expecting to see anything out of the ordinary, and froze. "Holy hotness!" she gasped.

It was blessedly clear which man standing by the baggage carousel was a Marine. He was the Hollywood version of Marine, too — tall, broad, and so corded with muscles beneath the short sleeves of his black t-shirt that all she could do was blink for a few seconds. His dark hair was clipped short on top and shaved on the sides in what she knew was called a high-and-tight style. He had one of those firm, take-nothing-off-nobody jaws.

"Wow!" She had to remind herself to breathe when her gaze fell on the uneven pattern of scars plastering his forearms. Scars he was making no effort to hide. He wore them as effortlessly as the rest of his skin. They were simply a part of who he was.

"Wow is exactly the right word for him," her grandmother chuckled. "Come on!" She tugged Kristi's hand, towing her in the man's direction. "Looks like he has the time for an introduction, after all."

"What? You mean he already turned down your kind offer to play matchmaker?" Kristi tried to slow her steps, but her grandmother pulled her along with a surprising amount of strength for a woman her age.

"He wouldn't have turned me down if he had any idea how wonderful you are." Aimi Kimiko's tone was matter-of-fact.

"You are very, very biased where I'm concerned," Kristi informed her faintly. "Trust me."

Her protest fell on deaf ears, but that didn't keep her from trying one last time. "You can't just throw me at the poor—"

"Why, Mr. Hammerstone!" her grandmother trilled. "I thought you'd already left the building."

Kristi's steps came to an abrupt and awkward

halt at her grandmother's side. Her heart thudded anxiously as the soldier turned to face them.

His expression changed from surprised to guarded. "That was the plan," he bestowed a wry grimace on her grandmother, not quite meeting Kristi's gaze, "but it looks like the crew is running a little behind in unloading our baggage."

Her grandmother gave a musical laugh and rolled her eyes. "As long as all my suitcases make it, I'll try not to complain too loudly. I travel heavy, and it's such a drag when the airlines misroute my things. Goodness! On one of my trips to Paris..." She rambled on for so long about the perils of lost baggage that Kristi's sympathies kicked in.

Feeling like she was extracting an innocent fly from the silken clutch of a spider, she leaned closer to the soldier and held out her hand. "I'm Kristi Kimiko. Apparently, you made a good impression on my grandmother. Now you have to suffer the consequences."

His firm lips twitched as he turned his head, at last, to regard her. Her gaze clashed with his hazel one, and his smile disappeared. For a few seconds, the world around them faded.

And for the second time in the space of five minutes, Kristi had trouble breathing. His gaze was that powerful, that potent. It was infused with too many emotions to name, though she had no trouble recognizing the weariness and regret. It was the look of a man who'd seen too much and experienced too much. The look of a man who'd suffered.

She also recognized the glint of hopeless admiration and longing in his gaze. Not merely the occasional flirtatious glance she was accustomed to receiving. It was more than that. Just...more.

"Axel Hammerstone." His hand briefly clasped and released hers.

Kristi felt like swooning. His fingers were warm, his touch gentle — unexpectedly gentle — which was at odds with the rest of him. She knew with sudden certainty that his hands weren't always gentle. They were capable of far more lethal things than handshakes. He was a Marine, after all, and the scars scattered across his arms indicated he'd seen some action on the battlefield. Recent action. Or not-too-distant action, at least. Several of his scars were still pink and puckered, not the faded silvery tone they tend to get after longer periods of time had passed.

She drew a deep breath, forcing air into her constricted lungs. "How long have you been back from overseas?" she inquired softly.

Surprise flickered in his gaze and was quickly masked. "Six months." His tone was clipped and didn't invite further questions.

"Welcome home." She infused as much warmth into her voice as she could, hating how breathless and off balance she sounded. She wasn't some high school ninny who dissolved into blushes and giggles every time she laid eyes on a hunky man in uniform. However, it was hard to think with the way he was perusing her so intently. "I mean, this is home for you, right?" *Oh, my goodness! I've got to stop babbling!*

The lights above the conveyer belt flashed, and suitcases started to slide from the center like a baggage volcano.

Axel half turned away to watch the progress of the growing pile of luggage as it circled in their direction. "I went to high school here."

She blinked. It was an odd answer to her question. She glanced around them. For a guy who'd attended high school in town, it was pretty clear he was alone now. Where were his friends? His family? Were they estranged? Had they moved away? *A-a-a-and it's none of my business,* she sternly reminded herself.

They watched the suitcases continue to circle the conveyer belt.

"So where did you go to high school?" *Yep, I'm totally turning into my grandmother, butting every which way into this poor guy's business.*

Axel's gaze flickered momentarily back to hers. "Booker T. Washington." After a pause, he added, "And you?"

"Highland Park."

He smirked.

"What?" she demanded, knowing she was

smiling like an idiot. She was thrilled they were finally having a real conversation.

He shrugged. "I pegged you more for a private school kinda girl."

"No-o-o," she teased, flattered by the admiring light in his eyes.

He arched a single eyebrow at her. "Or the Irma Rangel Young Woman's Leadership School."

"Now, you're just ragging me."

"I'm not." He chuckled but didn't elaborate.

"Well, what gave you the idea I was either private school or leadership school material?" she demanded, unable to let it go.

He reached for a pair of camouflage duffel bags, treating her to a delicious view of his flexing biceps. His eyes were twinkling as he set them down. "Don't forget I met your grandmother."

Kristi laughed. "Okay. You may have a point."

He nodded. "You should have heard the set-down she gave the pilot about our bumpy landing."

"Say it isn't so!" she groaned. "Did he try to defend himself, or did he have the sense to keep quiet and take it on the nose?"

"The latter. His co-pilot laughed, though."

"There's one of my grandmother's suitcases." Kristi made a dive for the bright red leather bag moving past them. It was one of the three pieces she was supposed to be watching for.

"I've got it." Axel reached around her to lift it from the conveyor belt.

"Thank you." She hated how breathless she sounded. "Got those football arms, huh?"

"Ha!" He rounded on her. "That's such a stereotypical statement. Big guy. Must have played football." His expression deepened to a glare. "There are other activities in high school, you know."

Her lips parted in surprise. "Of course! I mean, yes, you're right. I'm sorry."

"It's like asking if you were an honor roll student, because of your last name." He cast a sideways glance at her. "Or a cheerleader, because you're cute."

Cute! You think I'm cute? "I *was* on the honor roll," she confessed ruefully. "And the math team." As well as the valedictorian of her class. "No cheerleading." *Which is probably why I'm still single at the age of twenty-five. Not even a serious boyfriend.*

"Wow!" He burst into guffaws. "That's—wow! Seriously? I was just messing with you."

"Seriously." She made a face at him. "Complete nerd." Her face felt hot, and she wanted to dissolve straight through the floor.

He looked at her, as in *really* looked at her. "Well, you were right about me, too. I played football seven years straight. All through middle school and high school."

It was her turn to glare. "You're awful!" He'd really had her going for a minute there.

He winked at her. "No, actually, I was pretty good at it."

"Of course you were," she muttered, unable to believe how much she'd let his teasing ruffle her composure.

He lifted two more military-grade duffle bags from the conveyor belt and, without asking, nabbed her grandmother's last two red suitcases. He set them down in front of her. "Three MVP trophies and one shut-out season. We won the state playoffs my senior year. Best year of my life." For some reason, that fact made his smile disappear.

"Congratulations," she said softly, wondering why the best year of his life seemed to be making him sad.

"Yeah, congratulations," he echoed bitterly.

"Axel," a man shouted. "Axel Hammerstone?"

Their heads whipped around in unison. Kristi took a stumbling step back as a man with an enormous camera made a beeline in their direction. A bevy of people followed in his wake. One of them was a woman in a navy business suit, carrying a microphone.

The press? Kristi stared in shock at the logo on their equipment. They represented a prominent news station. It took a few more seconds for her to regain enough composure to shove her grandmother's suitcases out of the way.

"Well, that looks exciting. What did I miss?" Her grandmother, who'd been fiddling with her cell phone a few strides away, rejoined her.

Kristi shook her head. "I'm still trying to figure that out. One second, Axel and I were talking, and the next second..." She stared at the growing crowd. People were actually pulling out their cell phones to take pictures of him. A few college-age girls in skin-tight yoga pants and swooping necklines huddled close to him to take selfies. Another cameraman from a different news station materialized. Seconds later, airport security arrived with whistles and megaphones to break up the crowd and usher them outdoors.

"I need to get you out of here." Kristi hastily collected her grandmother's luggage, buckling a few pieces together so she could pull them along piggyback style. Soon they were rolling from the airport parking lot in her Fuji white Land Rover, one of her grandmother's many lavish gifts. It was certainly out of her price range, considering her dog handler's salary.

A deep rumbling sound made her duck her head to peek through the top of her windshield. A pair of helicopters were hovering overhead, their television logos emblazoned brightly across their tails.

"What is he? A Medal of Honor winner?" she

muttered. *Because I was just chatting with him at the airport like he was a normal guy instead of congratulating him.* She was ten shades of mortified. Her only comfort was the fact she wasn't likely to ever see him again. A thought that was accompanied by a crushing amount of disappointment. Which was an awful lot of feelings to have about a guy she'd only met briefly…

"It's not the Medal of Honor," her grandmother mused, tapping on the face of her cell phone. "It says right here that Axel Hammerstone is the proud owner of a Purple Heart, though there's talk about nominating him for some other awards."

Kristi didn't know if she was more surprised by her grandmother's announcement or the fact the woman actually knew how to do a google search on her phone. Electronic gadgets had always mystified her. Not to mention she was pushing eighty.

"A hometown hero, huh?" No wonder all the pretty girls had been thronging him in the airport. *While all I did was talk about high school grades and football with him. Boring!*

"So it appears. Oh, my!" Her grandmother scooted her reading glasses higher up her nose. "The article also says he was raised in foster care. Never got adopted. How sad!"

"Foster care!" Well, that explained why Axel Hammerstone, hometown hero, didn't have any family members present at the airport. It was because he had no family. Kristi shivered, unable to imagine such a thing. Then again, that could have been her life after losing her parents to a deep sea diving accident nine years ago, if she weren't fortunate enough to have the world's most amazing grandmother. Aimi Kimiko had opened her home to Kristi without question and finished raising her.

"I know, right? But he managed to stay in Dallas for middle school and high school, where he met his best friend, Marcus Zane. They joined the Marines at the same time and... Oh, dear!" Her grandmother sucked in a breath and fell silent.

"Oh, dear, what?" Kristi exploded after a few seconds. "Oh, dear, the stock market hit a new low? Oh, dear, your favorite hair salon is going out of business?"

"No, sweetie." There was no answering laughter in her grandmother's voice. "Marcus didn't make it home. He, ah...didn't survive the explosion, and Axel..." She cleared her throat. "Sounds like he was shot up pretty badly. Both legs. I guess that explains the limp." Her voice grew hushed. "He was so badly burnt that they sent him to that big military medical center in San Antonio. He just got released." She glanced up in awe. "We met an honest-to-Pete real American hero today, Kristi."

Got it. Loud and clear. Kristi suppressed a moan of misery. *And while I was cheerfully making conversation with him, exchanging what I thought were innocuous high school stories, I was actually breaking his heart all over again by forcing him to relive the tremendous loss of his best friend.*

Later that night, Kristi was unable to sleep in the bedroom her grandmother reserved exclusively for her only granddaughter in her Dallas townhome. Kristi generally spent Sunday evening through Friday morning at her cabin on the grounds of the Texas Hotline Training Center, a few hours south of Dallas. Someday she would secure a more permanent place for herself, but she was in no rush. The current setup worked really well for both her and her grandmother. They were super close — all that was left of the Kimiko family, in fact. It was why Aimi Kimiko was forever (and openly and shamelessly) playing matchmaker. Her biggest fear was leaving Kristi alone in the world someday.

Not that Kristi wasn't capable of surviving on her own. Lots of people had to survive on their own. Like Axel Hammerstone, for instance. She stared out the window at the stars, wondering where he was staying for the evening.

A wounded warrior without a family or a home. A man who'd only hours ago been released from a specialized medical care facility. A hunky football player who'd won a bazillion trophies for playing sports — enough awards that he'd probably been scouted by a college or two. Instead, he'd chosen to selflessly serve his country. A choice that had gotten him shot, burned, and nearly killed. A cause that had claimed the life of his best friend.

With a sigh, Kristi rolled to her side and pulled her pillow over her head. She'd never been one to believe in instant attractions or magical mumbo jumbo, but she was having an unusually difficult time getting Axel Hammerstone out of her mind. The way he'd looked at her with such hopeless longing. The gentle, cherishing way his hand had touched hers.

Logic told her that they would have never hung out in high school. They were too different. As an athlete — a wildly gorgeous one, to be more precise — he would have been running with the popular crowd, while she remained firmly anchored in the nerd herd. She was glasses and braces. He was football jerseys and cheerleader magnet material.

Funny how life had taken her in an entirely different direction than mainstream academia. She'd never ended up using her master's degree in research science. Instead, after attending a random search and rescue demonstration at her university's campus, she'd pursued the one thing that had finally given her peace following the tragic loss of her parents. She was training men and women in uniform and their rescue dogs how to save lives. She was doing something that would never make her rich, but it felt worthwhile every time her feet hit the floor in the morning.

That was the one thing she had in common with Axel Hammerstone. Just like she'd foregone the opportunity to land a higher-paying job with her two degrees, he'd probably passed up the chance to play college football in order to serve his country.

"I get you," she muttered into the darkness. "I get you in ways that most people never will." When she finally drifted off to sleep, a very tall, very broad, very scarred soldier with melting hazel eyes haunted her dreams for the rest of the night.

CHAPTER 3: FAMILY REUNION
AXEL

It took a few covert military-esque maneuvers for Axel to shake the last of the paparazzi — not an easy task for a limping soldier without a vehicle to his name, bearing four oversized military duffles in addition to his backpack. They contained all his earthy possessions.

He debated whether to head straight to the cemetery or find a hotel first — preferably one that served a free breakfast. It was early October, right smack in the middle of the off season, so it shouldn't be too difficult to renew his reservation one night at a time. Plus, it meant he could easily make a run for it if the news stations caught up to him again.

He was still shaking his head at the way no less than three television stations had interviewed him before he'd left the baggage claim area. *Man!* For the first time in his adult years, he was glad he didn't possess a home address or a cell phone number. Maybe he'd take his time acquiring those essentials. It might not hurt to stay off the grid for a while longer until all the hoopla died down.

He set his bags down at the curb, rubbing a hand over his stubbled jaw as he looked for the next taxi to flag down. *Didn't even think of shaving this morning.* He'd been too tangled up in the head over the thought of returning to Dallas. He didn't know how long he'd stay. It wasn't as if he had any real ties here. Not anymore, anyway, now that Marcus was gone. His memories of Marcus were what had brought him into town, though. He wanted to pay his respects one last time before drifting on. He owed Marcus that.

Digging through his biggest duffle bag, Axel unearthed a baseball cap. He mashed it on his head and pulled the brim low over his eyes. After a moment of consideration, he dug out a long-sleeved blue and white plaid shirt and buttoned it over his t-shirt. Then he reached for his sunglasses, since the media seemed bent on turning him into a blasted celebrity. He preferred the solitude of anonymity for what he was going to do next.

Not that he considered himself to be an actual celebrity. He couldn't, for the life of him, figure out why a handful of news stations found anything about him to be interesting. If he had to condense his life into a few headlines, it would read very differently from all the hometown hero nonsense they were spouting. Something along the lines of: *Local guy joins the Marines, gets shot, barely survives, fails to save his best friend, and returns to Texas a broken man.*

Shaking his head, he waved down the next taxi and was soon cruising toward the Dallas - Fort Worth National Cemetery. He'd have the rest of the day to find a hotel room. *Might as well get the toughest part of my trip over with first.*

Along with a handful of other soldiers during the Kandahar ambush, Marcus Zane's body had never been recovered, though a half melted piece of his dog tags had. The damage from the bombs and ensuing fire had been extensive, and it wasn't exactly easy for the U.S. military to pick their way through the debris in an enemy hotspot.

Sadly, this meant that nothing more than a headstone was present at Marcus's cemetery plot. Axel could only imagine how difficult it had been for his family to grieve without so much as a body to lay to rest there.

The Zanes had done what they could, though. According to a local news article he'd read online, they'd buried him with full military honors — including a twenty-one gun salute followed by a fellow Marine playing Taps with his trumpet. Axel both wished he could have been there and was thankful he was not.

Today was a far better day for him to pay his

final respects to Marcus, alone and unannounced. He walked with his head bent down, lugging his bags and hoping not to attract any attention. There didn't seem to be many visitors milling around. Though it was approaching the dinner hour, the sun was still beating relentlessly down. Probably too hot for most folks to brave a stroll through the cemetery, which was fine with him. He wasn't looking for company.

It didn't take him long to locate Marcus Zane's plot, since it was located in the newest section of graves. Axel's steps slowed as he approached the simple gray headstone. It was inscribed in all capital letters.

MARCUS J. ZANE
SNCO-7
U.S. MARINES
OPERATION ENDURING FREEDOM

BELOW THE DATES of his birth and passing were the simple words...

NOT FORGOTTEN

MOVED BEYOND WORDS, Axel tossed his bags in a pile. Then he took a knee in front of the stone and bowed his head. There were so many things he wanted to say to his friend, starting with a plea for his forgiveness. *I'm so sorry, brother. So sorry I couldn't save you. So sorry we didn't make it home together like we swore we would. I didn't deserve to live more than you did. Not even a little.*

He wasn't sure how long he knelt, only that the sun eventually stopped beating down so fiercely. A light breeze picked up, riffling across the cemetery grounds and making the dying blades of grass flutter.

Axel finally found his voice. "Semper fi," he said beneath his breath, standing and saluting the headstone.

"Oorah!" a male voice intoned quietly from behind him.

Shocked, Axel whipped his head around to find Marcus's father standing a few feet away. Tears dampened his dark face, wetting the sharp angles of his cheekbones. He was a tall man, almost as tall as Axel, but not quite as broad. He wore a gun metal gray pinstripe suit and one of those ridiculously bright colored shirts he seemed to own an endless supply of. Today, it was a rich shade of pistachio with a zany tie that probably would've won a ribbon at a modern art festival.

"Been waiting for you, son. Figured you'd eventually show up." Edgar Zane regarded him somberly.

Axel finished turning to fully face him, hating the way he nearly stumbled in the process. Looked like he was going to spend the rest of his life wrestling a bum leg.

"I'm sorry," Axel muttered, ducking his head. *I shouldn't have come.* He hadn't considered the notion he might be intruding on someone else's grief.

"For what?" Mr. Zane demanded. "For not returning Olivia's calls?" Olivia was his wife. "She's been worried sick about you," he continued sharply. "We all have."

Worried about me? Why? Axel was still unable to meet the gaze of Marcus's father. He'd figured no one in the Zane family would be able to stand the sight of him, everything considered.

"It's not your fault that you survived the war when our son didn't, you know."

Axel choked and tried to cover it with a cough.

"Did you really think we wouldn't understand how hard this is for you?" Edgar Zane made a sound of disgust. "You've been a friend of our family for sixteen years, Axel Hammerstone. S*ixteen* years, son. Now, get over here!"

Axel had been cracking at the seams for months, but Mr. Zane's words finished shattering him. Nodding, he wordlessly walked into the man's embrace. All the grief he'd kept bottled up exploded, and he finally wept.

Edgar Zane wept with him.

They were like a pair of trees swept up in a storm, bent just shy of snapping in two — stretched well beyond what one person was capable of enduring alone.

Somewhere in the tortured corners of Axel's mind, he was forced to acknowledge that this was what he'd needed most. To grieve and to share his grief with someone who understood. Someone who cared for Marcus as much as he did.

When the storm inside him finally subsided, he tried to take a step back, but Edgar Zane refused to let him go. "I just got you back, Axel. You can't take off again. Not yet." He pounded Axel on the shoulders and hugged him more tightly. "Olivia would strangle me in my sleep if she found out I'd run into you and failed to bring you by the house. No, I take that back. She wouldn't even wait until I'm asleep. She'd do it in broad daylight."

Axel's shoulders stiffened. "I can't, sir." Visiting Marcus's house would be too much like stepping on his late friend's shadow, like colliding with his ghost.

"Yes, you can, soldier. So, suck it up." Mr. Zane's earlier supply of sympathy seemed to have run out. "I happen to be far more afraid of my wife than I am of the likes of you. That means I'm not taking no for an answer."

"What about Kiera?" A note of desperation crept into Axel's voice. Kiera was their seventeen-year-old daughter. How would she feel about having him pop up unannounced? More importantly, how would she feel about seeing him show up without her brother? They'd been like two peas in a pod, traveling to and from the airport together during holiday leave and such. This was the first time Axel had made the trip back alone.

Mr. Zane patted Axel's shoulders again and finally stepped back. "If you insist on knowing, she's furious with you." He pulled out a white handkerchief and mopped the dampness from his face.

Axel dashed the backs of his hands over his eyes, then shoved them in the pockets of his jeans. "That's understandable." *I guess.* It wasn't like they were related or anything. He'd always assumed the only place he had in her life was that of her brother's friend. And now that her brother was gone, Axel had no idea where he fit in with her family. If anywhere...

"Is it?" Marcus's father sounded mildly incensed. "It would've taken you five minutes to respond to her get-well card. Less time than that if you'd simply picked up the phone." He made a huffing sound. "It was handmade, by the way. She spent hours on it."

A surprised chuckle worked its way up Axel's throat. "That's why I'm in the doghouse? For not writing back?"

Marcus's father shook his head at him. "Not sure why you're laughing. It's a pretty big mistake, in her book."

Huh. In all the time Axel had worried about what the Zanes would say or do the next time they saw him, it had not once occurred to him that they'd be this upset over his prolonged silence. Fortunately, this was something he could fix. Or so he hoped... He wasn't exactly an expert on how to smooth a woman's feelings after ruffling them.

"Yep. That's why you're in the doghouse, son." Mr. Zane marched around him to pick up a pair of his duffle bags. Then he angled his head toward the road. "Car is this way."

With a shrug of capitulation, Axel grabbed the remaining duffle bags and his backpack before falling into step with him. Now was as good a time as any to go apologize some more.

The wind picked up, whipping at their clothing. He had to press a hand to the top of his baseball cap to keep it from flying off.

"After facing my women this evening, you're probably going to wish you were back overseas doing simple things like hunting down terrorists, but I've got my money on your survival."

Axel cast a sideways glance at Mr. Zane, amazed that he was making a joke out of it. "Are they really mad at me for not writing?" As opposed to being alive when Marcus was not?

"Madder than hornets," Mr. Zane affirmed in a cheerful voice.

"But your wife and daughter are so sweet!" Axel couldn't picture them angry.

"As sweet as they come when they're not mad at you." Mr. Zane chuckled. "Speaking of sweet ladies, you got yourself a girlfriend or what?"

Axel stared, wondering when he would've found time for that, in and around all of his convalescing. "Not unless a chance encounter with a hot chick at the airport earlier counts." His voice was dry.

"Did you get her number?" the man shot back.

"Ha! You sound just like—" Axel bit off the words, groaning inwardly.

They reached Mr. Zane's car. It was a sleek black Lexus that fit its bank manager owner perfectly. He tossed Axel's duffles in the trunk and waited for Axel to toss the rest of the bags in before slamming the lid shut. "Where do you think Marcus got all of his charm, son? Chip off the old block." He winked at Axel as he strode along the side of the car to open the driver's door. "All aboard!"

He drove to a ritzy gated community that made Axel think they'd driven onto a movie set. The homes were all brick and the yards were well manicured. Sidewalks lined both sides of the streets, and lush summer foliage blossomed along the walkways around the three lakes they drove past.

"You moved," Axel noted in surprise. This neighborhood was a far cry from the humble white two-story Marcus had grown up in.

"That we did," Mr. Zane noted proudly as he parked in the driveway and stepped out of the car. "It took us a while to save up for it, but Olivia has had her eye on this neighborhood for over twenty years." He shook his head. "She'd been patient, and it was time."

His cryptic comment about the time made Axel wonder if Marcus's passing had anything to do with their decision to move. Was it part of their grieving process? Their way of leaving some of the old memories behind — at least, the ones that were too painful to face every morning?

He didn't have long to mull over such questions before a high-pitched shriek filled his ears. An older, taller version than what he remembered of Kiera streaked in his direction down the long brick sidewalk leading from the front porch. "Axe! Is it really you?" A blur of long dark hair, skinny legs, and cut-off jean shorts flew into his arms.

He caught the teen and swung her around and around, half-laughing and half-weeping. "When did you get so tall?" By the time he set her back on her feet, he was ready to wipe his eyes again.

"About the same time you got so mean."

To his shock, she drew back one slender hand and administered a resounding slap across his cheek. "That's for not writing, and this one is for..." She drew back her hand a second time, but Axel caught it and held on to it.

"Whoa!" He adopted what he hoped was a pitiful expression. "I just got out of the hospital."

Her expression turned incredulous. "You are so *not* playing the sympathy card with me."

He chuckled. "Eh, well, I thought it was worth a try, since your dad informed me that I'm in the doghouse."

Without warning, Kiera's sass turned to tears. She threw herself back into Axel's arms, sobbing hysterically.

He patted her shaking shoulders and looked over her head, aghast, at her father. *A little help?*

Mr. Zane merely shrugged. "Told ya." He ushered them up the sidewalk toward the front door, or tried to.

It wasn't easy for Axel to lead the emotionally distraught Kiera toward the house. She was plastered as tightly to him as a cocklebur caught in dog's fur, but somehow he managed. Almost.

Right before they reached the front door, she stepped directly into his path and shoved at his chest with both hands. "Don't you ignore us like that ever again, you hear?"

"Okay." He held up his hands in surrender. "Okay." His eyes were damp again. The fact that she genuinely cared about him touched him deeply. He should have never allowed his own grief to come between them the way he had. The Zanes deserved better. He could see that now.

"Good." Kiera's mocha lashes were drenched with dampness as she slid her arms around his middle, much more gently this time. "You're the only brother I've got left, Axe," she choked.

He hugged her back, pressing his lips to the top of her head. *I have a sister.* It was a crazy, wonderful feeling. *Thanks to you, Marcus.* Even in death, the guy was still giving, still saving, still making Axel's life a thousand times better than it had been before they'd met — during football tryouts the summer before they started the sixth grade.

Axel raised his head, swimming in so much nostalgia that it took a few seconds to register the fact that Olivia Zane was standing in the open doorway of her home. Her slender, dark arms were crossed, and her almond eyes were edged with flint.

Edgar Zane stepped her way to kiss her on the lips. "Go easy on him, love. He's been through a lot."

"So have I," she returned in a tart voice.

Mr. Zane shot an apologetic glance over his shoulder before stepping around her to enter the house. It was one of those *I tried* looks.

"Well, look what the cat dragged in," Olivia noted after her husband disappeared. She uncrossed her arms and raised her perfectly manicured eyebrows in a challenge. Then her expression softened. "Did you save a hug for me, or has Kiera used them all up?"

Kiera stepped back and gave Axel a shove toward

her mother. "Go face the lioness. I warmed you up for her."

He could've cared less at this point if Olivia Zane had been brandishing weapons. He was too over-the-moon with the knowledge that this amazing family cared for him — far more than he'd given them credit for.

"I'm sorry I didn't write," he muttered, jogging up the steps and leaning in for a hug.

"Or call," she snapped as her arms closed tightly around him.

"That, too. As Mr. Zane already pointed out, I'm not very well trained. Don't have a lot of female influence in my life." Yeah, he knew he was playing the sympathy card again, but it was the only card he had in his deck.

"Nice save." She pressed her face to his neck, and he felt the trickle of dampness against his skin.

"I thought so," he muttered thickly.

"It's so good to have you home, Axel." She drew a shuddering breath. "You don't know how long I've prayed for this day, or how hard."

"I had no idea." His voice was rough.

"You're the answer to those prayers, my precious boy," she sighed against his neck.

Um, wow!

Her voice suddenly changed. "Are you hungry?" She raised her head, smiling brightly despite her tears.

A chuckle rumbled its way through his chest. "I'm a guy."

She smoothed her hands over the front of his shirt. "Well, I happen to have a pot roast, a pan of collard greens, some rice, and a pecan pie that are going to get cold if we don't skedaddle into the dining room."

"Yes, ma'am!" His mouth was already watering. Giving her a two-fingered salute, he followed her inside.

Kiera caught up to him in the hallway and bumped her elbow against his. "So who's the special lady in your life these days?"

The glare he shot at her was only half mocking. "What's up with all the interrogations about my love life?" He reached over to tap her on the nose.

She swatted his hand away. "No girlfriend, huh?" She rolled her eyes. "Did Marcus teach you nothing?"

He was amazed by how easily her late brother's name rolled off her lips. He shouldn't have been, though. Moments later, it became very apparent just how much the Zanes were keeping him in the forefront of their thoughts and memories.

A large canvas painting of Marcus in full dress uniform adorned their dining room wall. It was spectacular.

Kiera joined Axel in front of it. "He was drop-dead gorgeous. That's why all the girls were always going nuts over him."

"Yep." Axel slung an arm around her shoulders. "And that, my dear, is the real reason I'm still single. He was my wing man. I never stood a chance with the ladies when he was in the room."

She giggled. "Okay, now you're exaggerating."

"Maybe a little." He squeezed her shoulders, his thoughts roving to the stunning Kristi Kimiko.

"Aha! I recognize that look." Kiera stabbed a finger against his chest. "There *is* somebody, isn't there?"

"No." He caught her hand and lowered it to her side. "What's it to you, anyway?"

She cocked her head sassily at him. "You have to ask? Boy, do you need work!" She made a face. "It's my job, okay?" At his puzzled expression, she rolled her eyes. "As a sister...to know things about you..."

"Well, that's some fine writing for you," he grumbled, but he couldn't have been happier at her confession. *Man!* He'd missed this. The many meals and visits he'd enjoyed with the Zanes in the past had been the high points of his teenage years.

Olivia and Edgar Zane waited until dessert had been served and Kiera had been called outside to hang out with some friends at the lake. Then Olivia leaned across the dining room table to touch Axel's hand.

"I know this is hard to talk about, but we were

told you were the one with our son at the very end. Is it true?"

Axel nodded, meeting her pained gaze. "I was, ma'am."

She swallowed hard, her eyes filling with tears. "Was he hurt bad?"

"No, ma'am." Axel hunched his shoulders over the table, searching for the right words. "We rolled over a cliff right before our armored truck blew up, so the worst of the explosion missed us." They'd felt the heat from the flames, though, and the sting of debris raining down on their shoulders.

"Dear heavens!" she murmured.

Edgar Zane reached for his wife's hand.

"The only thing that kept us from falling the rest of the way was the grip I had on a bush growing from the side of the mountain." He still couldn't believe the foolish little piece of foliage was what had ultimately saved his life. He drew a few deep, steadying breaths as he relived the toughest part of what happened next. "It took me a moment to realize Marcus was holding on to my ankles. I couldn't feel my legs by then. I'd taken too many bullets." He cleared his throat. "I tried to hook my elbow around the bush, so I could free a hand to pull him up, but..." He stopped and cleared his throat. "Marcus shook his head at me. I think he realized that I, er...wasn't in any condition to..."

Olivia Zane caught her breath sharply and gave a short whimper. "Did he say anything?"

"Simper fi," Axel said softly. "Then he let go."

She nodded, lips trembling and shoulders heaving with silent sobs. It was several minutes before she spoke again. "You know what this means, don't you, Axel?"

He had no idea what it meant. All he knew was that returning to Dallas hurt far more than he ever imagined it would, but it was a brand of hurt he could deal with. In fact, he welcomed the pain. He mattered to these people, and they mattered to him. He should have never been afraid of facing them — of hurting and grieving together.

Olivia reached across the table to clasp his hands in hers. "Look at me, son."

He met her gaze, no longer making any attempt to mask his emotions. She was the closest thing he'd ever had to a real mother, and he was pretty sure there wasn't anything in the world he wouldn't do for her if she asked.

"It means you belong to us now. We're bound by blood. Marcus's blood. You're no longer just a friend of the family. You *are* family."

His heart constricted as he met her gaze. "Okay, Mom," he choked

She nodded, beaming at him through brimming eyes. "That's more like it." Then she pushed back her chair. "I'll go get the guest room ready."

"Wait. What?" Axel glanced at Edgar Zane for help. "I, ah…couldn't possibly impose like that." Since he hadn't notified them of his travel plans, they hadn't been expecting him.

Olivia paused her exit from the room to glance over her shoulder. "Why not? Did you already find a place to stay?"

"No, I'm staying at a hotel." Her look of disdain made him smile. "It's temporary, just until I get things figured out."

She gave him a withering look and finished sailing into the hallway. "No son of mine is going to stay in some ratty public hotel, and that's that." Her voice wafted back to him from the stairs as she ascended to the second story.

Mr. Zane chuckled at his aghast expression. "Don't look at me. You heard your mother."

Axel laughed as he rubbed both hands over his face. "Guess I could hang out for a day or two, but I seriously can't do this for long."

"Why not?"

Axel blew out a breath. "I've been on my own for a long time, Mr. Zane."

"That's Dad to you, son."

Axel chuckled again. "I'm twenty-six-years-old. I'm a big boy now."

"Not arguing that." Edgar Zane raised his black brows. "But do you really think Marcus would've spent his first night home in a hotel?"

Axel shook his head, grinning. "You're not going to let this go, are you?"

Marcus's father grinned back. "No, because I kinda like being a married man. My wife says *jump*, and I say *how high*." He settled back in his chair and crossed his hands behind his head. "Different topic. I know it's only your first day back, but have you given any thought about returning to the firehouse?"

"I honestly haven't, but it's not a bad idea." Axel grimaced in contemplation. Serving as volunteer firefighters was something else he and Marcus had done together. "It would certainly give me something to do while I figure out what comes next."

"It would."

"I have something to tell you." Axel hadn't bothered sharing what he was about to share with anyone else yet. Quite simply, he'd had no one to tell until now.

"I'm listening."

"I've been taking online classes for the past few years, but..." He held up a finger. "I finally finished my four-year degree in Fire Science last month."

Edgar Zane's hoot of exultation made Axel jolt in his seat. It also brought Olivia Zane running.

"What in the world?" Balancing a stack of neatly folded white towels and wash cloths in her hands, she shook her head at her husband. He'd leaped from his seat at Axel's announcement and was now dancing a jig around the dining room table. She turned to Axel. "Do you know what's gotten into him?"

He stood to sweep into a gallant bow in front of her. "Just finished telling him he's looking at a brand new college graduate. I earned my bachelor's degree in Fire Science."

She gave a shriek of delight, threw the stack of towels over her head, and ran his way to throw her arms around him.

CHAPTER 4: FLIRTY PHONE CALL
KRISTI

One month later

Kristi blew her dark bangs from her eyes, fanning her face. It had been an unusually hot September, and October wasn't showing much more interest in cooling off. Sure, the mornings were a little cooler in the high 50's and low 60's, but it kept shooting up into the 80's by the afternoon.

"I'm so ready for fall," she grumbled, knowing no one was likely listening to her.

"That's what my fiancée said this morning," Brick Mulligan noted with a grin. He was the senior K9 Search and Rescue Handler at the Texas Hotline Training Center, a specialized school that prepared men and women across the state to join the prestigious TEXSAR first responder organization. Once they became credentialed members, they could then be deployed in times of need at the request of statewide law enforcement, fire departments, and emergency management agencies.

Kristi chuckled. "The truth, according to God and Carrie Collins. I'm in good company."

"That you are. I'm still going to give you the same answer." Brick stepped inside his office and returned with a folder, which he dropped on her desk. "One night soon, boom! It's going to get Texas frigid on us, and you'll be wishing for beach weather again."

"Not this gal." She fluttered her hand at her face again and reached for her mug of iced tea. "I started praying for snow a month ago. What's this?" She patted the blank manilla folder. "Big, furry secrets about the underbelly of the training center, huh?"

"You wish! It's actually our list of new recruits reporting for class next Monday."

"Oo, gimme!" She eagerly opened the folder. "Poor unsuspecting souls to put through our newest set of diabolically torturous training exercises." She rubbed her hands together in anticipation. She loved her job — every second of every day. She was the luckiest woman in the universe that the training center had decided eight months ago that Brick could use a full-time understudy.

"I've created a monster," Brick muttered dryly.

"Now, Officer Mulligan!" she protested sweetly. "If I recall, our whole good cop, bad cop routine during instruction time was totally your idea." Plus, it was a heck of a lot of fun for both the instructors and the trainees.

"Point taken." He waggled his brows at her. "I'm just wondering when I'm ever going to get a turn at playing the bad cop."

She made a snarling sound and pretended to scoop up all the papers on her desk. "When you pry my speaker's notes from my cold, lifeless fingers."

"Like I said," he rolled his eyes at her and disappeared back inside his office, "I've created a monster."

"Harsh," she commented to his shoulder blades. "Can you believe what I have to put up?" This she addressed to Cyclops, Brick's K9 partner. Cyclops was a German shepherd he'd brought with him from his past life as an officer in the Black Mountain PD in North Carolina. "Then again, look who I'm beefing at. I mean, you have to work more closely with him than I do. Poor you!" she mourned.

"I heard that," Brick called from his office.

"You were supposed to, officer," she retorted sweetly. Her eyes ran swiftly over the list of names for their new recruits. "Oh. My. Goodness!" One name in particular might as well have been written in fat red letters with a ginormous marker for the way it practically jumped off the page at her.

"Now what?" Brick popped his head around the corner again.

"Did you see the names on this list?"

"I'm the one who handed you the folder, remember?"

"Axel Hammerstone." She pointed with her pen. "He's like a mega hometown hero in Dallas."

"So?"

"Purple heart. Parades in his honor. Lots of television interviews. I'm pretty sure they sold out of the hottie-hot firemen calendars he and his compadres at the firehouse posed for to raise money for charity." She should know. She owned two copies and had failed to pick up a third — not for lack of trying. "It'll be like having a celebrity in our midst." Her heart thudded a thousand beats a minute at the thought of seeing him again. At the absolutely insane fact that he was about to become her student!

"Yeah, well, I'm sure your bad cop routine will take him down a peg or two if he needs it."

Hoping her voice didn't sound as shaky as she felt, Kristi pointed to the top of the list. "Here's another one that jumped out at me. A recruit called FirstName LastName. Is that some sort of joke?"

Brick snorted and threw up his hands. "You do realize there's professional help out there for people like you, right?"

"Heartless!" She tossed her head and went back to work. There were files to open for each new recruit, as well as for their K9 partners. The trainees were required to either bring a dog of their own to class or work with one of the company dogs the training center kept in-house at the kennel.

But trainees weren't allowed to bring just any ol' mutt to class. They had to provide proof that each animal was healthy via an affidavit from their veterinarian, that they were up-to-date on their shots, and that they'd been electronically chipped for security purposes. With fifty new recruits in each monthly rotation of classes, that spelled a lot of paperwork for her and Brick. As his understudy, she did most of it, of course. Thankfully, the on-site veterinarian office shared the online database and helped maintain it.

The office phone rang, and Kristi shot a pleading look in Brick's direction. "I'm so swamped with paperwork, I'm going to have to don my snorkeling gear to avoid drowning," she moaned.

"You called me heartless," he pointed out without looking up. He was crouched in front of Cyclops, going through their afternoon rehearsal of basic calls and signals.

"And harsh," she muttered, typing furiously on her keyboard. "Don't forget harsh."

"I could live up to my name, or..."

"I'm begging you." *Make it stop!* She scowled at the phone. "In my head, I'm on my knees!"

"Well, in that case." He rose from his crouch and took a few steps back to reach for the phone on her desk. "K9 Search and Rescue Handler office. This is Officer Mulligan speaking. How many I help you?"

As he listened, a slow grin stole across his handsome features. He waggled his eyebrows playfully at her.

"Please don't hand me the phone. Please don't hand me the—don't do it!" she hissed, baring her teeth at him.

"He asked for you, Miss Kimiko." Brick searched her face with interest and curiosity.

"Who asked for me?" she whispered loudly. "I wasn't kidding about my snorkeling gear! I'm drowning here."

He waved a hand and covered the mouthpiece before answering. "Nobody important. Just a firefighter/EMT from Dallas named Axel Hammerstone."

"Okay, I deserved that. Here." Shaking her head, she reached for the receiver. "Just remember. Paybacks are tough."

Brick merely put his hands on his hips and watched her as she spoke into the phone.

"Kristi Kimiko speaking. How may I help you?"

"Kristi? It's Axel. Axel Hammerstone."

Her mouth flew open.

"Priceless," Brick chortled softly.

Oh. Em. Gee! Kristi mouthed at her boss.

He shook his head and turned away, chuckling, "Where's my camera when I need it?"

"I don't know if you remember me," Axel continued, "but we met at the Dallas - Fort Worth International Airport about a month ago."

"Oh, right! Yes, I remember meeting you." She'd dreamed about him every night since then and daydreamed about him when she wasn't sleeping. The brooding, wounded warrior with the soulful hazel eyes... Her heartbeat tapped a few hundred extra beats per minute at the memory.

Brick whirled around and shook his finger at her with a you-were-holding-out-on-me look. She was never going to hear the last of it.

"Good! Well, it sounds like I'm about to become one of your students. What are the odds of that?" He gave a rueful huff.

"About a million to one," she supplied, smiling. *Which I so don't mind.* Having him on the other end of the line felt like an early Christmas gift.

"So, uh, I've done volunteer firefighter work in the past, but I'm new at doing this stuff full time. And to make things even more exciting, my department highly encourages all their employees to join TEXSAR. So, here I am, embarking on a month of search and rescue training."

"Well, congratulations on your new job!" *Wow!* Only home a month and already he'd landed a new position. All the hometown hero publicity had probably helped in that regard.

"Thanks, I think. I'm still working to prove myself. Only time will tell if the department made the right choice in taking a chance on me."

She snorted. "They chose the right guy. I think

your Purple Heart speaks for itself." So did his humble attitude, which she found utterly endearing. She'd met her fair share of men in uniform, and humble usually wasn't the highest on their list of attributes.

He was silent for a beat. "Well, anyhow, I'm kinda late to the dog party. In fact, I just acquired a retired police dog this afternoon. I'm hoping it's not too late to get him added to my file. That is...it's okay for me to bring him on Monday, right?"

"I'll need his up-to-date shot records, a veterinarian affidavit of good health, and proof of a security chip."

"Got two out of three, but I can show up for class on Monday with the affidavit in hand."

"That'll work." *I hope.* She'd have to ask for an exception to the policy, since the paperwork was supposed to be cleared through their veterinarian office before each recruit was allowed to start training. She hoped she could talk Brick into approving it.

"I'm relieved to hear it. I was worried I might have to leave ol' Diesel behind."

"Is that your dog's name?" She swallowed a giggle, in case he was being serious.

"Yep. He spent the last five years working for the Dallas PD."

"Am I the only one who sees the humor in this?" A giggle escaped her. "A dog named Diesel working with a guy named Axel."

"Not at all. I've been taking heat from the guys about it for two straight hours. They don't hold back."

"You can always try cotton balls," she suggested with another giggle.

"Come again?"

"Cotton balls. For Diesel's ears, so he doesn't get his feelings hurt."

Axel snorted. "Uh, when you meet Diesel, you'll see why that's not a problem."

"Big dog, huh?"

"Three inches taller than me," he shot back.

"Yeah, I'm definitely going to need that affidavit." She grinned at nobody in particular. "This is starting to sound like one of those leg-pulling fish stories."

"You'll see," he warned.

"And the man doubles down instead of folding. Nice play. Just for that, I'll wait until Monday to call your bluff. What's his breed?"

"Golden retriever."

"Age?"

"Six and change."

"How much change?"

"He was born on the 4th of July."

"Can he salute the flag?"

"He can sing Yankee Doodle in three different keys, ma'am."

I'm totally falling for a guy I've met only once.

Smiling like an imbecile, Kristi asked a few more questions about shot dates and lab tests. "Okay. I've got his file open for you. It would make my life a lot easier if you would scan and email his electronic chip and shot records...like today." *Right this minute, preferably.*

It was nearly closing time on Friday, and Kristi's grandmother was expecting her for a late dinner that was beginning to look less and less like it was going to happen. Then again, Aimi Kimiko would likely be quick to forgive when she heard the reason Kristi was begging off their dinner date.

"Consider it done. I'm walking toward the scanner right now."

Thank you very much! "You're the best."

"That's what all the ladies tell me."

She snickered, hardly believing she was flirting with Axel Hammerstone! "Says the humble, pin-up fireman with a heart for charity."

"Ah. You saw the calendar."

"I did." *Be still my heart!* But still wasn't even close to describing how her heart was behaving right now. More like a jackhammer on steroids.

"And?"

"I applaud your efforts. It was for a good cause."

"Aw, come on! At least tell me if it's hanging on your wall," he wheedled.

Yes, it is, and no way am I admitting it! "That'll cost you extra. I'm already working overtime." Or she would be five minutes from now, not that she intended to document it.

"I'll pay up," he said quickly.

"Sorry. My boss would never approve overtime. Oo, did you just hear that dinging sound?"

"It was more of a cracking sound. That was my heart breaking."

She caught her breath and had to swallow — hard — before composing her next comeback. "No, I'm pretty sure it was a dinging sound. Yes, now I'm very sure." She tapped a few computer keys. "It was your email coming through, as requested. If you'll just hang on a second longer, I'll verify the attachments arrived safe and sound."

"I must confess, this is the first time any woman has shown more concern for my dog's well-being than she has for my own," he notified her in a caressing voice.

"Oh, no! It's not a lack of concern." Her voice shook despite her effort to keep things light. "It's just that all humanoid types of medical records are handled by our clinic, which I'm so sorry to say is closed for the weekend."

"So you *do* care? At least a little?"

"That's classified." Translation — she was crushing on him twenty-four seven.

"Guess I have my work cut out for me before I ask you out."

On a date? Every last word in the English

language flew out of Kristi's head. For once in her life, she was fresh out of comebacks.

"Right. Too soon." He gave a gusty sigh. "Well, I've got a whole month to wear down your resistance. I'll just have to try again."

She still couldn't think of a single blessed thing to say in return. It was one thing to be privately crushing on someone. It was another thing entirely for him to show up and start crushing back.

"Hey, are you okay?" He sounded concerned.

She pressed a hand to her heart. "What?" Her voice was barely above a whisper. She cleared her throat and tried again. "Did you say something? I thought you hung up five minutes ago."

"Okay, I deserved that." He chuckled. "I'm hanging up now, Kristi Kimiko, but I'm really looking forward to seeing you on Monday. Oh, and..." he paused and lowered his voice conspiratorially, "if you want me to sign your copy of the charity calendar, just bring it to class. I'm sure we can work something out." He disconnected the line.

What just happened? She stared at the telephone, utterly stunned. The guy of her dreams — the shy, reserved, and broody wounded warrior she remembered from the airport — had just called her and acted spontaneous, humorous, and romantic.

Sheesh! Who are you, and what have you done with the real Axel Hammerstone? Not that she didn't like the new version of him. She did. Her hands shook as she painstakingly transferred the key details in the files Axel had scanned and emailed to the master file she'd created for his SAR dog.

What unnerved her the most was the fact that their flirt-fest had been a true clash of minds, one in which Axel had no difficulty keeping up with her. Her brain worked on one speed — overdrive. It was full of dates and numbers, facts and details. She possessed a photographic memory and such a high IQ that she scared away most of the datable guys in her life. Being extraordinarily smart was a definite strength on the job, but it was a clear flaw when it came to her social life. It was something she continuously struggled to hide with witty repartee, hoping to come across as entertaining as opposed to a complete brainiac.

But for the past few minutes on the phone with Axel Hammerstone, she hadn't once felt the pressure to hide her true self. With him, she could just be real.

Brick strode from his office with the strap of his leather briefcase slung over one shoulder. "You get Hammerstone all squared away?"

"I believe so." She didn't dare look up from her computer screen to meet her boss's gaze. Her emotions were in way too much of a tangle. "Everything except the affidavit. He just adopted a dog this afternoon. Soonest he can have it to us is Monday morning, in person. Is that going to be a problem?"

"What kind of dog?" Brick asked coolly. He paused in front of her desk.

She risked a quick glance upward. "Retired police dog. Five years of SAR experience. He said the original owner is taking an extended vacay in Europe and didn't want to kennel him or keep him out of the field that long."

Brick slowly nodded. "I take it, you've confirmed he's chipped and his shots are up to date?"

"Yes and yes."

"Then I only see one problem."

"Oh?" Her heart sank.

"Next time, clear it through me first."

Kristi nodded. As much as she was convinced she'd made the right call, Brick was right. Ultimately, any exception to policy was his decision, not hers. "I'm sorry."

He waved away her apology and rapped his knuckles on her desk. "It's personal, isn't it?"

She had two choices — pretend ignorance or be honest. She settled for something in the soggy middle. "I've only met him once, Brick."

"That's not an answer."

"Fine. I don't know." She folded her hands and met his gaze. "What do you want from me, Brick? To sit this month out because I know one of our students? Turn in my resignation?"

"Heck, no!" he exploded. "The last thing I want is to lose you, Kristi. You knocked my socks off during the interview, and you've exceeded my expectations ever since. We need you here at the training center. I'm just trying to stay ahead of something before it becomes a problem."

"Okay. I like him," she confessed. "I barely know him, but he made a very good first impression, whereas most people don't. So, yes, it's a little personal."

His lips twitched. "Now we're getting somewhere." Then he sobered. "Here's a pop quiz. What would you do about me if our roles were reversed? Bear in mind our company's reputation, as well as the integrity of the services we deliver."

"Let me deliver instruction. How I feel about any particular student won't affect the quality of my work. I'm very good at what I do."

"Agreed. I'm the one who recommended you for a raise."

"Thank you." She grimaced. "My objectivity, however, might be skewed when it comes to evaluations. I shouldn't be grading Axel Hammerstone's work. Make sure he's on your panel, not mine."

"I fully intend to, Kristi Kimiko. Just wanted to make sure you and I are on the same sheet."

"We are." She was grateful to work for someone so approachable.

"Alright. You passed the quiz." He gave her a mock salute. "See you in sixty-three hours."

"It's five past five." She glanced at her watch. "So

technically, we'll be seeing each other again in sixty-two hours, fifty-five minutes, and—"

"Unless you take into account the fact that you always show up five minutes early."

Her jaw dropped. "I'm rubbing off on you. That's kinda scary."

"Get out of here!" He waved both hands at her, grinning. "Shoo! Go start your weekend before the numbers change."

CHAPTER 5: GROUND RULES
AXEL

Axel had to call in a favor to get Diesel's affidavit of good health completed after hours. It cost him no less than two autographed copies of the firemen calendar for the veterinarian's two daughters, plus a promise to serve as the keynote speaker at an upcoming charity ball the man's wife was organizing.

It was a steep price for a single signature on a single form. However, Axel was anxious to show up on the first day of class at the training center with a real search and rescue dog, so he didn't have much choice. Besides, it only made sense to train with the dog he'd be handling when he returned to Dallas, and Diesel was a dog he could picture himself working with long-term. Lastly, if he was being honest with himself, he also hoped to impress Kristi Kimiko. Showing up with a search and rescue dog who had more experience than most of the recruits in the room couldn't hurt that mission.

He traveled down to the training center the evening before, not wanting to fight Dallas traffic the following morning, and secured a dog-friendly hotel in town. The evening was young after he checked into his room, and the weather was decent, so he decided to take Diesel for a jog. Afterward, he brought the dog back to the hotel to feed, water, and kennel him. It sounded like his last owner had been very strict on routines. Axel planned to follow them to a T. He would only make small, gradual changes as needed to suit his personal schedule.

After getting the dog settled, he showered and threw on a plaid shirt and pair of comfortable jeans. Since he was in town early, he figured it might not hurt to start learning his way around. He'd find some place to eat dinner, and he'd do it in Texas style. That meant throwing on a belt with a big buckle, boots, and a Stetson. It inevitably reminded him of the old days when he, Marcus, and their Marine buddies were cutting up the dance floor on one of their Friday night outings.

Well, maybe not quite like the old days. Yeah, it was Sunday, but he was alone this time. Walking along Main Street, his gaze fell on a winking neon sign with a single word spelled out — *Diner*. That sounded promising. The place might even have a jukebox in the corner. Not to mention he was a big fan of breakfast food any time of the day.

As he pushed the door open, a set of bells hanging at the top of it gave a cheerful jingle.

A fortyish woman in a pink and white striped dress with her hair in a kerchief looked up from behind the counter. She was mixing a pair of ice cream shakes in two tall glass tumblers. Chocolate mint, from the pale green shade of them. "Sit anywhere you want, sugar. I'll be with you shortly."

His mouth watered as she added brownie crumbles to the top of the shakes and sprayed on a generous dollop of whipped cream. *May have to order one of those with my meal.*

He scanned the room, which was nearly empty, and no wonder. It was nearly eight-thirty, well past the dinner hour. There was a retired couple on one side of the room and a police officer perched at the bar. His gaze landed on a familiar fall of dark hair next.

No way! His heart pounded at the realization that Kristi Kimiko was sitting alone at a booth on the far side of the room. The only reason she hadn't seen him yet was because she was facing away from the door.

A dozen good reasons why *not* to approach her filled his head. For one thing, she was about to become his instructor for the next month. Secondly, she had gone curiously quiet on the phone when he'd joked about asking her on a date. Well, it had started out as a joke, anyway. But the moment he'd said it, he'd realized just how badly he wanted to do exactly that. She was smart, kind, funny, and beautiful — definitely a woman he wouldn't mind getting to know better.

Shaking his head and debating what to do about her presence in the diner, he noted a jukebox resting against the wall to his right. *Perfect!* He dug in his pocket for change and moved over to it to study the play list.

He'd done his fair share of dating, but he'd never had trouble refocusing his attention on his job the next day. That's what was different about Kristi. After a chance encounter with her in the airport, he'd been unable to get her out of his mind.

Marcus wouldn't have approved of the way he'd let her simply walk away in the airport, though the arrival of the paparazzi had made it difficult to continue their conversation. Unfortunately, he'd been pretty messed up in the head that day – still drowning in guilt about Marcus. However, the Zanes had been a tremendous help in easing that guilt in recent weeks. No, they'd done more than ease his guilt.

Man! He shook his head in wonder. They'd become the family he'd always wanted. They'd given him hope that he might actually have a shot at getting back to living a normal life. What's more, he now had a home address and a cell phone number. Despite Olivia Zane's protests, he'd secured an apartment down from the firehouse, though he visited them as often as he could.

Being his own man again was a game changer. *I'm date-able again.* He grinned at the thought and selected an oldie but goodie country love song. At first, the music poured softly from the machine. Then it grew louder and fuller, filling the diner.

You amaze me, the male vocalist crooned. It was the perfect background music as Axel strode across the diner and paused at Kristi's table.

"Hi."

She glanced up at him, her dark eyes rounding in surprise. They were as beautiful and expressive as he remembered. Eyes that mirrored her kindness and razor-sharp wit. At the moment, they were also swimming with countless unanswered questions.

He couldn't help wondering if he stood even the slightest chance at coaxing her into going on a date with him at some point.

"Mind if I join you?"

"Not at all." She fluttered a hand at the bench across from her.

He slid into it, removed his Stetson, and set it on the red vinyl upholstered cushion.

She glanced around them before spearing him with a puzzled look. "How did you find me?" Her voice was low and hushed.

"Fate." He smiled and picked up a menu.

"No, really."

"Really." He perused the menu and decided to forgo the breakfast entrees in lieu of a double burger and curly fries.

"You're a Marine, so you probably have excellent tracking skills. Not to mention, you're training in search and rescue. So, I'll ask again. How did you find me?"

He laid down his menu and glanced around for their waitress. She was bustling in their direction. "Maybe I'm pursuing you." His eyes twinkled into hers.

She gave a breathless laugh. "Why?"

He arched his brows at her. "Isn't it obvious?"

"Isn't what obvious?"

He angled his head at the woman approaching them. "Saved by the waitress." He didn't want to cripple their conversation with too much talk about dating too soon. "I'm ready to order. Are you?" He eyed the half-empty glass of iced tea in front of her.

Their waitress must have arrived in time to hear his question. "She said she wasn't hungry." A disapproving expression rode her round, motherly face. Her name tag read *Janie*. She reached for the pen behind her ear and held it over her pad, eyeing him expectantly.

"Well, I am. I'll take your quarter pounder and fries, medium well, with all the trimmings." Axel shot Kristi a challenging look. "If you change your mind, it's my treat."

She narrowed her dark gaze on his. "I don't usually eat the evening before a new training session. Too much on my mind. But if you know of the perfect energy boost, soldier boy..." She let the words hang between them.

Sounded like stress to him. He smirked. "As a matter of fact, I do." He turned to Janie. "Bring her a fried liver sandwich with a side of frog legs and—"

Janie, who had started to write on her pad, burst out laughing.

Axel waggled his eyebrows at Kristi. "You gotta problem with my recommendation?"

She rolled her eyes, then glanced up at their waitress. "No liver or frog legs. Just a simple grilled chicken wrap on a separate check, please."

His heart lurched with disappointment. Her message was clear. This was not a date, which was probably for the best. He'd needed to reign it in, since she'd be instructing him in class tomorrow.

She straightened in her seat, tossing her glorious dark hair behind her shoulder. "And maybe one of those berry burst side salads, if you still have the ingredients on hand. I know it's getting late."

"We do, love." Janie winked at Axel over the top of her pad. "You come back any time, handsome, you hear? You're good for business."

He grinned at Kristi as the waitress walked away,

unable to resist one more small jab of fun. "She called me handsome, in case you missed it."

A delectable shade of pink tinged her high-boned cheeks. "Axel! What are you really doing here?" She twirled her straw in her glass, making the ice clink against the sides.

He decided it was time for the truth. "Actually, I'm staying at a hotel nearby. Thought I'd travel into town early and get the lay of the land. Got hungry, saw the diner, and you just happened to be here when I walked in." He held up two fingers. "Scout's honor."

"Uh-huh." The color in her cheeks deepened to a delicious shade of rose. "Well, when you walk into my class tomorrow, I'm not going to go easy on you."

"I'm counting on it."

"As much as I've enjoyed meeting you, we're going to have to keep things professional there, alright?"

"During business hours?" he shot back. Before she could answer, Janie materialized with a fizzy soda and served it to him with a flourish. "Ahhhh! Guess I forgot to order a drink, but you read my mind perfectly."

She chuckled. "I added a dash of cherry syrup."

"If I wasn't already spoken for, I'd ask you to marry me."

She smoothed a hand over her hair and smiled at

Kristi. "I like this one, sugar. Don't let him get away like the last—"

"I'd like a refill, please," Kristi interrupted, lifting her half-empty glass of tea.

"Sure thing, sweetness!" Janie took it from her with a knowing smirk.

"Hmm." Axel folded his arms and leaned his elbows on the table. "Kind of sounded like Janie was—"

"I'm your instructor, Axel, and apparently you're spoken for."

"All I meant was that my interests are already engaged elsewhere." Though he kept his voice teasing, it was truth.

"We can't do this right now." Her voice was firm. "I'm sorry, but we can't."

Right now? "That's not a no." He leaned forward to sip on his soda, also so he could look more deeply into her gorgeous eyes.

"Besides our instructor-student status, we barely know each other."

He held her gaze steadily. "I'd like to change that."

The worry in her gaze didn't fade. "I think it might be wise to establish a few ground rules before tomorrow."

His grin widened. "Still doesn't sound like a no."

"No dating and no public displays of affection during the program. Training center rules."

His shoulders relaxed at the realization she was only giving him a no for now. "I can live by the rules, Kristi Kimiko. Just so you know, it doesn't change the fact that I'm interested."

"The only way you're going to pass this program is if you give it a hundred percent of your time and attention. I don't want to take away from that."

"You won't." If anything, the fact that she was considering dating him would motivate him. He sighed in appreciation when Janie returned with two steaming plates of food on one arm. She had Kristi's requested refill in her other hand.

Kristi waited until she walked away before continuing, "Because we know each other, I've already made arrangements for someone else to evaluate your performance in the coming weeks."

"Oh?"

"You'll be on Officer Brick Mulligan's panel for grading purposes. He's my supervisor."

"Thank you."

"For what?"

"For giving me hope."

She gave a breathy chuckle. "Actually, it's the only way to protect the integrity of the company I work for."

"Which wouldn't be necessary if there was nothing between us."

"If you say so." She glanced away. "I'm not even

sure why we're having this conversation. We're nothing alike, Axel."

His heart pounded at the implications of her words. It was all the proof he needed that she'd been thinking about him as much as he'd been thinking about her. "I hear that opposites attract."

"Only in the movies," she sighed. "You and I?" She shook her head. "If we'd attended high school together, a guy like you would have never even noticed a girl like me."

"Maybe. Maybe not." He drummed his fingers on the table. "I've always subscribed to the theory that things happen for a reason." Granted, he was still trying to make sense out of a few unexpected twists and turns that life had dealt him. "What if you and I were supposed to meet *after* high school? First in the airport, and again tonight."

"Do you really believe that?" Her expression turned inexplicably sad. "About things happening for a reason?"

"I'm trying to." He glanced away, thinking of Marcus. "Sometimes it's the only thing that gets me through the day." He huffed out a breath of resignation. "The faith that God's still in His Heaven and all's right with the world, as Robert Browning once said."

"So, you're a poet," she said softly.

"Actually, I'm a realist, but I find comfort in wise old sayings."

"Maybe we're not so different, after all." Her voice grew hushed. "Today is the ninth anniversary of my parents' tragic passing during a diving accident, and I still have trouble making any sense of it."

Ah. It was the real reason she was having trouble eating this evening. Axel almost felt guilty for pushing her to order food. Almost…

He stood and walked to her side of the booth. "Scoot over."

"I thought we just finished establishing some ground rules."

"Just do it, please."

She moved over and leaned back against the wall, putting as much space as possible between them. There was a weariness in her gaze he hadn't noticed before.

"I don't remember my parents, Kristi, so I can't begin to understand your loss. All I can say is, I'm sorry for it. Sorry that you're sad tonight. Not sorry, however, that you don't have to be alone with your sadness." He slung his arm across the back of the booth. His fingers rested less than an inch from her slender shoulders.

"So, here we are." Her eyes glinted with emotion. "Two orphans offering comfort to each other."

"Hey, you're the one who said we couldn't kiss." He lowered his arm from the booth to drag his plate from the other side of the table. Then he lifted his burger with both hands and took a bite. "Wow!" he muttered around the food in his mouth. He chewed and swallowed. "This is good. You should try it."

"Your burger?" A giggle escaped her.

"If you want." He held it out to her.

"Heck, why not?" She leaned closer to take a nibble.

"You call that a bite?" He raised his brows at her. "That wouldn't keep an ant alive."

"I'm really not very hungry."

"Want me to order you a shake?" He took another bite.

"What part of not hungry don't you understand?"

"Ice cream will make you feel better."

"That's a myth."

"Then it's a myth I happen to like." He waved Janie down and put in an order for a gigantic chocolate sundae shake. "Two spoons, please."

"You betcha, sugar." Janie hurried off, beaming her approval at him.

Kristi studied him from beneath her lashes. "What happened to you?"

He grew still. "What do you mean?" It was such a vague question, he didn't know if she was referring to all the scars on his arms and hands or what.

"You were a broody soldier the first time we met. I could barely get you to talk. Then yesterday..." She toyed with the straw in her glass again. "It's like you'd completely changed."

He nodded. "That's an easy one. Some longtime friends adopted me."

"You got adopted?" Her voice rose to a squeak. "At your age?"

"Unofficially, yes." He was enjoying keeping Kristi off balance and hoped it was distracting her from her sadness. "In every way that matters. The Zanes are pretty incredible. Even insisted I start calling them Mom and Dad."

"The Zanes," she repeated carefully. Her smile dimmed. "I take it they're the parents of Marcus Zane?"

"Yeah." Apparently, she'd read about Marcus's passing. "It's one of those rare cases, I guess, where something good actually came out of something tragic."

"I'm happy for you!" she exclaimed warmly.

"Really?"

"Really, really." She pressed her lips together ruefully. "And maybe a little envious."

"Hey, you have your grandmother. She seems incredibly nice."

"She's the best." For some reason, Kristi sounded sad. "But she's all I have left, Axel."

"Not true. You have me now."

Kristi idly stirred her tea with her straw, seemingly lost in thought.

"Hey!" He turned to face her expectantly. "We could share, you know."

"Share what?" She glanced up in bemused askance.

"You have a grandmother. I have adoptive parents. Oh, and I have a sister, too."

"A sister!"

He nodded happily. "Kiera Zane. She was just a little thing when Marcus and I joined the Marines. She's seventeen now. Well, she's about to turn eighteen two Sundays from now. They're having some big hoopla birthday block party thing that I'll be expected to attend. That is, if the training center will allow me to leave for a few hours."

"They might allow it on a Sunday," she conceded, sounding doubtful.

"Good, because I'm under very strict orders from Olivia Zane — my mom," he explained with a wink, "to bring a plus one."

"Axel!" Kristi cried softly. "I thought we agreed we weren't going to start dating yet."

He liked the sound of *yet*. "Yes, but we have since moved on to the topic of sharing families. I'll share the Zanes if you'll share your grandmother." He shrugged and gave her what he hoped was an innocent look. "It's a three-for-one deal. You're making out like a bandit."

"I don't know what to say."

"How about a yes?"

"How about an I'll think about it?"

Disappointment flooded his mouth. "Well, it's better than a no."

"Axel," she sighed. "I want to. I really do."

"Good." Relief replaced his disappointment.

"It's just that..."

"Tomorrow you're going to be busting my chops in class."

"Something like that."

"I can handle whatever you plan on dishing out, Kristi." He polished off the rest of his fries and chased it down with a mouthful of soda. He'd stared down the barrel of death itself. More than once. There was nothing in her dog handler training course that could be worse than that.

"Once a Marine, always a Marine, huh?"

"Oorah!"

Their gazes locked and held for a breathless moment, both of them asking and seeking, both of them wanting and longing.

Janie reappeared with their decadent shake. She slid it across the table to them. "Enjoy, my dears!"

Axel eyed the enormous dessert in appreciation and reached over to remove one of the spoons. It was covered in vanilla ice cream with bits of brownie and chocolate syrup clinging to it. He held it out to Kristi, grinning a wicked challenge. "You first."

"I can't believe I'm agreeing to this." She swiped the spoon from him and popped it inside her mouth.

"Because you find me irresistible?"

"More like relentless."

He reached for the other spoon and helped himself to a generous bite. "Are you feeling better yet?"

"A little."

Janie returned and slid their food ticket, face down, in Axel's direction.

"No. No way!" Kristi made a dive for it, but Axel snatched it up and held it away from her.

"This is not a date," she insisted, waving her ice cream spoon at him. "We agreed to some ground rules."

He angled his spoon against hers in a dueling pose. "Yes, we did, and you have nothing to worry about." He fluttered the food ticket at her for emphasis. "This is just me being a gentleman by not asking Janie, who's already put in a long day, to go to the trouble of separating this into two checks. Altruism at its finest."

"You're impossible to reason with," she grumbled, stabbing her spoon back into the shake.

"Not true. I can be a very reasonable guy." He watched her take another bite, glad to see she was finally eating. "I'll even consider letting you pick up the next tab if you promise to take another bite of your sandwich before you wrap it up."

"You'll consider it, huh?" She closed her eyes and made a moaning sound as she was savoring the ice cream.

"Yep."

Her eyes opened, and there was a softness in them he hadn't noticed before. "Meaning you're not going to let me pay, are you?"

"Nope." He laid his spoon down and stood.

"How is that being considerate?"

He reached for his Stetson and propped it back on his head. "It's in the fine writing." He spoke in a low voice so that only she could hear him. "You agreed to let me take care of you the moment you agreed to be my girl."

"But I didn't agree—"

"All you said was not now." Whistling, he strode for the cash register to cover the tab for one of the most enjoyable evenings of his life. "And you happen to be a girl I think is worth waiting for."

CHAPTER 6: TEACHER VS. STUDENT
KRISTI

Kristi lay awake in her instructor cabin at the training center, which was never a good thing the night before a new class showed up for orientation. She needed all of her wits about her when the latest batch of recruits marched with their K9 partners into her classroom.

But all she could think about was Axel and his kind, understanding eyes, his teasing voice, and the emphatic way he'd called her his girl. Did it mean they were technically dating even though they'd agreed not to? *Gah! This is so confusing!*

She rolled onto her back and stared at the ceiling. Axel was so different from the other guys she'd dated — not that she dated very often. He flirted, yeah, but he hadn't tried to put any moves on her. Nor had he balked too loudly at her no kissing and no dating ground rules, though he seemed to be finding ways around them pretty quickly.

She slung a hand over her eyes, wondering what she should do about his invitation to go as his plus one to his sister's upcoming birthday party — his *unofficial* sister. She could think of several smart reasons to say no, but that didn't change the fact that she wanted to go.

Lord, give me wisdom! If she was being honest with herself, it wasn't just her job keeping her from saying yes. It was the long string of losses she'd suffered — her parents, her grandfather, her bestie who'd passed in college from a brain tumor, and her grandmother sure wasn't getting any younger. As for her boyfriends? They all found a reason to break up with her nerdy self, eventually.

If she agreed to date Axel Hammerstone, she'd be exposing her heart all over again. And as nice as he was, she could think of far more cons than pros for dating him. For one thing, his new position as a firefighter/EMT was a few hours away in Dallas, while her dream job was right here at the Texas Hotline Training Center. What was the point in starting a long distance relationship, when statistics said most of them were doomed to fail?

Her other concern was that he was hot, plain and simple — the hottest guy who'd ever shown any romantic interest in her. It was only a matter of time before she completely nerded out on him and scared him away for good. *Shoot!* She might not even have to wait that long! She was about to find out if he could handle her bad cop instructor routine in just a few hours.

And boy, did she have a bad-cop-of-all-bad-cops surprise planned for her new recruits today! It was something she'd been mulling over for a couple of weeks, and Brick had given it his wholehearted approval. That was before she'd realized Axel was going to be in her class, of course.

Moaning out loud, she rolled from bed at the crack of seven, knowing she hadn't done much sleeping. At least, she'd been horizontal for a few hours, though. It was better than nothing.

She donned her standard black cargo uniform and pinned on her silver Texas Hotline Training Center badge. She was proud to be a part of a company with such a worthwhile mission. The job would never make her rich, but she had the satisfaction of knowing she was helping make the world a safer place, one search and rescue professional at a time.

She tugged her combat boots on next. Wearing them always made her feel like a soldier heading into battle. Then she tightly French braided her hair, rolled the tail up, and secured it with a stretch tie. Settling her THTC cap over it, she pulled it low on her forehead. She liked the way the cap cast a shadow over her eyes, adding to her no-nonsense appearance. A woman as short and petite as she was had to use every trick in her arsenal.

The training center's main auditorium was teaming with chatter and excitement when she took her place on stage with the other instructors. The new recruits filled the first several rows of chairs in the audience. It was their largest class yet — seventy-five bright and promising men and women from across the country, including one American soldier who'd been sent all the way from her MP unit in Iraq. The THTC owners were tickled to death at the opportunity to work with her and were hoping this would lead to a future training contract with the U.S. Armed Services.

Retired Colonel Ed Schwartz, their esteemed THTC commander, strode on stage with a sharp command to his staff. He advertised a bootcamp-type immersion experience, so he ran the entire program military style. At this command, the chattering of their audience fell silent as she and her fellow instructors snapped to attention — two neat rows of men and women standing shoulder-to-shoulder in their black cargo uniforms, feet together, arms at their sides, heads facing straight forward.

A second command from the Colonel had them moving in unison to a position the armed forces referred to as parade-rest. Their arms were bent akimbo behind them, one palm splayed atop the other on their lower backs, feet slightly apart, and their faces staring straight ahead.

Moving only her eyes, Kristi sought out Axel and found him sitting in the front row. Her heartbeat sped at the sight of him in his camouflage pants, a fitted sand-colored t-shirt, and matching combat boots. *Man!* He was a beautiful creature!

His easy-going smile from the evening before was gone. His features were stony and intent. She couldn't tell if he was looking at her or not. It was clear he hadn't come to the orientation ceremony to flirt with her; he'd come to train.

"Welcome to the Texas Hotline Training Center, new recruits," Colonel Schwartz barked. "At this time, your cell phones should be turned off and your full attention on the men and women standing on the stage behind me. For the next month of your life, your social media followers can trade cute kitty memes without you, and your email inbox can fill to overflowing. Your only task is to follow the instructions of the finest search and rescue instructor team in the nation, so you can get back to your regular jobs and start saving lives with the help of your K9 partners."

Axel didn't bat an eyelash throughout the colonel's tirade. However, his gaze did finally seek out and find hers.

Holy smokes! No dating. All business, she reminded herself fiercely, hating the way her insides turned all trembly at a single look from him. To her discomfort, he watched her the rest of the time Colonel Schwartz was introducing his second-in-command, Sandro Guerra. Sandro proceeded to outline the requirements of the course and displayed a map of the training center on the big screen overhead. The hulking Hispanic man lifted his remote control to flash through photos of the male and female dormitories, cafeteria, gym, kennel, hospital, and training center.

Axel's gaze flickered a few times to the images on the screen, but his attention always returned to Kristi.

"Each of you has a personalized instruction packet waiting for you at the booth in the back of the room," Sandro droned. "You'll be rotating through various phases of training at different times, and not all of you will receive the same instruction. Some of you will leave this facility as experts in bomb detection techniques, which happens to be my background. Hooah! Whereas others of you will be focusing on narcotics detection, water rescue, or arson investigations. All of you, however, will rotate through our bedrock dog handler course, where you will undergo state-of-the-art training in tracking and scenting."

He directed the students to go pick up their specialized packets next and gave them one hour to unload their belongings from their vehicles to their dorm rooms. "Your instructors will be ready to deliver your first lesson at the crack of nine. In order to successfully complete the program, your attendance is required at all times. No exceptions. Class dismissed!"

Only then did Axel drop Kristi's gaze. He swiftly tossed his backpack and an extra duffle bag over his shoulder, moved to join the flood of students filling the aisle, and strode with them to the back of the room.

She and Brick walked side-by-side to their instruction area. Except in cases of inclement weather, they met outside in a football-sized field. It was a massive training site for dogs. There were rows of canisters for tracking and scenting exercises, an overgrown section of field where yet more scent specimens were concealed, and a number of obstacles around the perimeter to test the strength and agility of the dogs. The rest of their instruction would take place in alternate locations throughout the training center — from the rubble of urban buildings to the lake where the dogs would engage in water rescue exercises.

Kristi jogged ahead of Brick to unlock the small metal storage building that rested on a concrete slab at the entrance gate to the field. She withdrew five bite suits. They were large padded bodysuits in the signature THTC black. Each was padded from the neckline to the hem line to protect trainees from puncture wounds — the kind inflicted by dog teeth. She hung them in a neat row on hooks outside the storage facility. On top of each clothes hanger, she hung a helmet with a face mask, similar to what a football player might wear.

Adjoining the storage facility was an outdoor kennel with ten separate cages. Earlier that morning, she'd relocated several of the facility's best trained dogs from the indoor kennel to the outdoor cages. She'd purposefully reduced their morning food rations to make them edgy for the coming exercise. Fortunately, they were well trained. They knew the drill and knew they would be fed immediately afterward.

The next hour flew by quickly as she and Brick finished preparing for their first lesson. Within five minutes of the designated class time, nine of the new recruits were present — seven men and two women. Kristi was fascinated to note that the soldier from Iraq was among them. Axel was not.

Kristi anxiously scanned the gravel road leading to their training site, but he wasn't there. She couldn't bear the thought of him showing up late or missing the training. It was grounds for immediate dismissal from the program.

Come on. Come on. Come on. She glanced at her watch several times as the dreaded countdown began. A mere thirty seconds prior to the deadline, Axel finally jogged across the field to join them.

She scowled at him, wondering why he was cutting it so close. Then she sucked in a breath at the limp to his gait. Was he in any pain?

She knew it wasn't very professional of her, but she allowed herself a brief moment to drink in his broad shoulders and bulging biceps. Gosh, he was gorgeous! She resisted the urge to sigh out loud in relief that none of their students were late. The first hurdle had been crossed. The program requirements would only get tougher from this point on.

Brick nodded at Kristi to indicate he was ready to begin. She took her place in front of the dog kennels and assumed the parade-rest position.

He faced their students with his hands on his lanky hips. "Welcome to Day One of our esteemed search and rescue dog training segment of the program. We know all of you have mastered the basics of dog handling, so we'll skip straight to the good stuff. Our first lesson was designed by Instructor Kimiko to my left, your right, as a confidence building exercise."

Two of the male students smirked. Kristi mentally marked them as her first two volunteers.

"How many of you are runners?"

All ten students raised their hands.

"Excellent. That means you've probably been chased by a dog a time or two in your life. Dogs sure love to chase runners."

There were several head nods and a few grins.

"It also probably means you've been bitten before, some of you more than once. Raise your hand if you've ever been bitten. Yep. Yep. Me, too. It's no fun, is it? Always results in doctor visits, rabies tests, and antibiotic injections."

Brick glanced over at Kristi to make sure she was ready. She gave him a single nod. He turned back to their semi-circle of students. "Anyone here afraid of dogs?"

This question was met with mostly blank stares. Nobody ever wanted to admit they were afraid.

"Okay. How about a healthy respect for how dangerous they can be, then?"

Axel's hand went up. A few others followed suit. The two smirkers smirked harder.

"Good. Everyone who's working with dogs should have a healthy respect for their capabilities. For the purpose of this class, dogs are your search and rescue partners, but they can also serve as weapons. Never forget that. Watch dogs, guard dogs, security dogs, patrol dogs, and search and rescue dogs have one very important trait in common. They can be trained to attack at your command."

At a subtle signal from Kristi, the dogs in the cages emitted a chorus of low, snarling growls from deep within their throats.

The smirks in their audience slipped. This was Kristi's cue that it was her turn to speak. She sauntered over to her boss to take her place by his side.

"Officer Mulligan said dogs are weapons. And just like any other weapon, you have to learn how and when to fire them. All the dogs you see in these cages behind us are trained to attack and even bite non-compliant individuals at the commands of their handlers. By non-compliant, I mean anyone who breaks and enters, attempts an assault and battery, or is guilty of any number of other crimes punishable by jail time. The dogs you brought with you, which are currently housed in the training center's indoor kennel, will be likewise trained to attack and bite in the coming days. But first, it's only fitting to give you a live demonstration of what we're talking about."

She pointed to the two men who'd smirked throughout most of the instruction so far. "You and you will pose as our first non-compliant persons. I need three more volunteers." It wasn't a punishment. She'd learned from experience that the quicker the students learned to take the program seriously, the likelier they were to succeed in the program.

The female soldier's hand went up. "You." Kristi waved her forward. "Who else?"

Axel raised his hand. She nodded at him, then scanned the group for her third and final volunteer. "Alright. Suit up and make sure your helmets are firmly clasped." She pointed in the direction of the bite suits. "I'll get the dogs ready. This is probably a good time to tell you they haven't been fed yet, so each of you in your bite suits will look as juicy as a

Hereford steak. I wanted to lather barbecue sauce on your bite suits, but Officer Mulligan vetoed my suggestion."

Her last comment was met with a single nervous chuckle from one of the spectator students.

"Okay." She waited until Brick had checked each student's suit and helmet for a snug fit. "For the purpose of this exercise, each of you wearing the bite suits is guilty of breaking and entering my warehouse. What you didn't realize, prior to this afternoon's crime spree, was that I have a pack of well-trained guard dogs patrolling my facility. The moment you realize your mistake (and that moment will be when you hear me blow my whistle), like any sane criminal who is not intoxicated by alcohol or strung out on drugs, you will take off running as hard and as fast as you can. If you can reach the double yellow spray paint lines before my guard dogs attack, they will assume you've jumped the fence and escaped from their reach. If, however, you fail to run fast enough, be prepared to engage them."

Axel's hand came up.

"What is your question, new recruit?" Kristi was pleased at how cool and impersonal her voice sounded.

"Are we allowed to fight back?"

It was a fair question, one that the toughest students always asked.

"You can try, new recruit."

He nodded gravely, while the two smirkers exchanged uncertain glances.

"All new recruits in bite suits, take your places on the nearest yellow line," she ordered crisply. A glance at Brick assured her he had the dogs lined up and their leashes removed.

"Alright. I hate to tell you this, but you just made the biggest mistake of your life by attempting to break and enter my warehouse facility." With that, she blew her whistle.

The runners leaped into motion, and the dogs flew snapping and barking after them.

Kristi felt an unholy burst of pride at the speed with which Axel ran despite his limp. Nevertheless, he was the first one the dogs attacked. One second, his arms were pumping and his legs striding in a forward motion. The next second, his entire body was flying through the air and being slammed to the ground.

The female soldier was slammed down next, and the other three men followed in quick succession. Kristi watched dispassionately as the dogs yanked their targets around like rag dolls for another few seconds. Then she blew her whistle to end the exercise. She and Brick ran forward to pull the dogs free.

It was an exercise a few of the dogs enjoyed a little too much sometimes. They didn't always let go until she and Brick had their hands on their collars.

While Kristi hustled the dogs back to their

kennels to feed them, Brick gathered the dazed group of "targets" around him and waved the five spectator students over to join the huddle. "Alright. How many of you are afraid of dogs now?"

There were more head nods this time, plus a few rueful chuckles.

"Right. Me, too. Besides building your confidence to handle hostile dog encounters, this exercise was designed to drive the point home that dogs are weapons. Learn how to fire them. For the next segment of our training, you'll proceed to the indoor kennel, put your dogs on their leashes, and report with them to the veterinarian's office. There they will receive a wellness examination to clear them for training. After our lunch break, you'll report back to this field with your K9 partner on a leash. At that time, we will commence the next phase of our training with a bite sleeve. Class dismissed."

Brick grinned at Kristi after the students removed the bite suits and walked in a huddle toward the cafeteria. "Nice job, Bad Cop Kimiko. Our introductory lesson never gets old. It's hands-on, engaging, and pretty stinking effective."

"Thank you." She folded her arms as she studied the dogs. "Way too many recruits come to class not understanding the full range of their dog's capabilities. I think this exercise puts that in a better perspective. At the very least, it wiped the smirks off of a few faces."

"Which you enjoyed way too much."

"A girl has to have her fun!" A gleeful chuckle escaped her. It was true. She enjoyed their introductory exercise more than she should, but Brick was equally guilty.

He sobered. "Hey, I think it's worth noting that Hammerstone had his attack dog pinned. Couldn't tell if you noticed."

"As in completely immobilized?" Kristi's lips parted in surprise. She'd never witnessed a student doing that before, and certainly not with Bruiser. He was a Doberman Pinscher with over six years of field experience, a dog fully capable of living up to his name.

"Yeah. Might want to have Bruiser checked out by the vet real quick. Just in case he's nursing an injury."

"Roger that," she murmured. *Unbelievable!* She'd call to set up the appointment right away.

"I got the impression Hammerstone was holding back, too. We're fortunate he understood the dogs were intended to survive the exercise."

"Survive?" she exclaimed, aghast at the implication.

Brick nodded, his expression as serious as taxes. "Otherwise, Bruiser might've sailed on a one-way ticket to the happy hunting ground. Hammerstone is the real deal. Once of those Marines whose bare hands should be registered as weapons."

CHAPTER 7: BIRTHDAY BASH
AXEL

Though the training center discouraged outside visitors and typically didn't allow their students to leave campus during their month of training, the commander discreetly made an exception for Axel to attend Kiera's birthday party. It helped that Edgar and Olivia Zane put the heartfelt request in writing, explaining how Kiera had lost Marcus during Operation Enduring Freedom and that Axel was the closest thing she had left in the world to a brother.

To avoid raising questions among his fellow students, Axel left his pickup truck in the student parking lot and ordered a cab to meet him outside the training center's gates.

He was unsurprised, but highly disappointed, at how little opportunity the training center had afforded him to interact with Kristi Kimiko. Though he caressed her with his eyes every chance he got, they enjoyed no time alone. There'd been no more dinner rendezvous at the diner, and not a single chance for him to confirm whether she was able or willing to attend Kiera's birthday party. As valuable as he found the search and rescue training, he couldn't wait until it was over, so he could officially start dating her.

He had the cab driver drop him off at his apartment, so he could change into a navy suit and a pair of cowboy boots. If he correctly recalled from his high school years, the Zanes were all about dressing up for their parties, so he didn't hold back. According to the formal invitation, this one had an Alice in Wonderland theme, and the dress code was semi-formal, or "quirky snazzy" as Kiera had been quick to inform him.

Since he had no clue what quirky snazzy amounted to, he decided to fall back on his tried-and-true look and go as a cowboy. He added a black and silver bolo to the collar of his white button-up shirt and a wide silver buckle to his belt. Then he snatched the birthday gift he already had wrapped from his chest of drawers. It was a crystal paperweight bearing the insignia of the unit he and Marcus had served in during Operation Enduring Freedom. With the gift tucked like a football beneath his arm, he hopped yet another cab to the Zane's home.

Kiera's party was in full swing by the time he

arrived. There was an enormous white and gold balloon archway over the driveway, an event-sized white party tent anchoring the front lawn, and a live band playing. The band members were decked out like various characters from Alice in Wonderful — the Queen of Hearts, the Mad Hatter, the rabbit, and the Tweedle brothers. It was every bit the epic block party the Zanes had promised it would be.

The moment he deposited his box on the gift table, Kiera danced up to him in a frilly lavender dress that made her resemble a sun-kissed version of Cinderella. A sassy hat, consisting of a trio of topsy-turvy teacups, rested atop her head.

She threw her arms around him, hugging him tightly. "You made it!"

"Hey, there, birthday girl." He hugged her back. "Of course, I made it." The Zanes had made sure of it. He was grateful that they had.

She tipped her face up to his with a mischievous look. "In about twenty minutes, I'm supposed to kick off the dancing. How's about us making it a brother-sister dance?"

"You're on." He stepped back to high-five her.

"Wait a sec!" She wrinkled her forehead as she glanced expectantly around them. "Where's that plus one you promised Mom you were bringing?"

"I'm right here." Kristi Kimiko's voice wafted softly their way.

Axel spun around in his boots, joy coursing

through his chest. "Wow!" He drank in the sight of her floor-length orange gown and her faux fox fur shrug. His breathing took on a rough edge. "You look amazing."

"Thank you. You clean up pretty good, yourself, cowboy." She turned to Kiera, who was staring at her wide-eyed, and held out both hands. "This must be the sister I've heard so much about. Happy birthday, Kiera!"

Kiera took her outstretched hands, looking dazed. "Thank you, Axel," she breathed. "You've been holding out on us." To Kristi, she murmured, "I want to know, and fully intend to find out, everything there is to know about my brother's stunning plus one, that I'm sorry to say he's told us absolutely nothing about. But for now, I'll settle for your name, vocation, driver's license number, and date of birth." Her dark eyes twinkled wickedly. "For the sisterly background check."

Kristi chuckled. "I'm Kristi Kimiko, an instructor at the Texas Hotline Training Center. Thank you for inviting me to celebrate this special day with you." She made a face. "I'll confess it's kind of nice to have an excuse to lay aside my combat boots for the evening."

Kiera gave an exaggerated gasp and slapped both hands to her mouth. "You're dating one of your teachers, Axe?"

"No-o-o," Axel and Kristi exclaimed in unison.

"Oh! Pardon the misunderstanding." Kiera held up her hands, laughing. "You see, the idea of a plus one—"

"I know what a plus one is, minx." Axel rolled his eyes for Kristi's benefit. "I'm kinda new at this big brother thing, but having a younger sister is turning out to be a royal pain in the backside."

"Why, thank you." Kiera gave him a princess-worthy curtsy.

"That wasn't intended as a compliment."

"I know, which all the more assures me that I'm doing my job as a sister." Her dark eyes continued to sparkle wickedly as she straightened and waved her finger beneath his nose. "Don't forget about our dance. I'll come back to collect you in a few minutes."

"Roger that." Axel gave her a mock salute that made her giggle.

"I like her," Kristi murmured as Kiera spun away from them.

"Yeah. Me, too. She's a handful, but she grows on you." After a short hesitation, Axel placed his hand against the small of Kristi's back and led her toward the refreshment table. They'd agreed to no dating or public displays of affection, but she hadn't precisely prohibited him from touching her altogether. To his relief, she didn't shrink or shrug away from his hand.

The food and beverages turned out to be no less spectacular than the rest of the party. A heart-shaped ice sculpture anchored the center of the table. On either side of it were enormous fountains of chocolate fondue and cheese for dipping everything from fruits, to vegetables, to crackers and pretzels. A three-tiered cake made of unevenly stacked clocks served as the birthday cake at the far end of the table. There were other finger foods galore, and a long line of flavored water dispensers floating with watermelon slices, mangoes, pineapples, lemons, and berries.

"What a spectacular party!" Kristi gazed around them in wonder. "My grandmother would approve."

"Does she like to entertain?"

"Does she ever!" Kristi chuckled. "She prefers smaller gatherings, though. Large crowds wear her out more than they used to."

"That's understandable."

"Don't get me wrong. She'd come to a gig like this. She just doesn't have the energy to plan and host something of this magnitude, herself, any longer."

Axel grunted. "I can't even imagine what all went into the planning of this thing. I suspect the Zanes went over the top for the express purpose of distracting Kiera. This is the first birthday she's had to celebrate without Marcus."

"It must be tough on all of them."

"It is. All of Kiera's silliness aside, you can see it in her eyes."

"An outsider would never guess. She puts on a good face."

"That's for her parents' sakes." He nodded. "She's a smart kid. She understands tonight is as hard on them as it is on her."

"I always wondered what it would be like to have a sibling," Kristi mused with a smile. "I'm starting to think it's a pretty amazing thing."

"Well, now you don't have to keep wondering. I agreed to share them, remember?"

"I may take you up on that offer yet." Kristi rested her hand on his arm, making him gaze down at her in surprise. Her hand looked so good, so right there.

"Oh, ah—" She laughed breathlessly and withdrew her hand. "I was just going to ask you to bring me a glass of that sparkling water."

"Which flavor?"

"Surprise me."

The moment he returned to hand her a bubbling glass of mango water, Kiera popped back up at his side. "Sorry, Kristi. Gotta borrow my brother for a few minutes."

Kristi cheerfully waved her glass of mango water at them. "Have at him. It's your birthday, kid."

"Thanks." Kiera wound her dark arms around Axel's arm and dragged him, laughing, toward the dance floor.

"She's really pretty, Axe."

"I am aware," he agreed, his gaze roving back to Kristi.

She fluttered her fingers at them.

"You gonna marry her or what?" Kiera demanded as the band struck the opening notes of their song.

"That's not a bad idea." He swung her around in a circle and dipped her, making her laugh.

"I thought you said you weren't dating anyone."

"Yet," he protested. "I'm not dating her yet. All in good time, sis. What's the rush?"

"I just want you to be happy, Axe. Is that asking too much?" She wrinkled her nose at him. "You get so moody sometimes that I worry about you."

Kiera danced him back to Kristi at the close of their brother-sister number. "Your turn," she sang out merrily.

"I see." Kristi set down her glass of sparkling water. "Far be it from me to turn down a special request from the birthday girl."

"Thanks! Though he's a keeper, it doesn't feel right to hog all of his attention, even on my birthday." Kiera nodded knowingly at Axel. She snapped her fingers at the band and made some motion with her hands that he didn't understand.

The band transitioned to a slower song.

"Nice." Axel gently drew Kristi into the circle of

his arms. "She really needs to work on the whole subtle thing."

"I like her just the way she is." Kristi rested her hands lightly on his shoulders. "She's everything a younger sister should be."

"You mean annoying?" He cuddled Kristi as close as he could, breathing in the faint scent of her perfume. She was so fine-boned and delicate, so soft and feminine. Everything about her entranced him, right down to the way her long, silky hair was brushing against the backs of his hands.

Kristi gave a soft chuckle. "I'm referring to the way she makes you laugh."

"Yeah, she's a nut. Always has been."

"So, there's something I've sort of been dying to ask you," Kristi announced suddenly.

He raised his eyebrows. "Yes. I will marry you."

She blushed and caught her lower lip between her teeth. "Sorry, cowboy. That wasn't the question."

He was entranced by the color blooming in her cheeks. "Too bad."

She cocked her head at him, humor gleaming in her eyes. "It's about the first day of class."

"Ah. The Marco Polo game with the attack dogs. It was a fun exercise. Pretty effective."

"So it's true." She shook her head in wonder at him. "Brick swore you had yours pinned."

"Brick?"

"Officer Mulligan."

"He seems like a nice guy. Is he my competition?"

"What? No!" Kristi playfully swatted his shoulder. "He's my boss."

"You're my instructor," he reminded.

"He's engaged to an amazing woman named Carrie Collins."

"Whew!" He dragged in an exaggerated breath of relief. Swaying gently with her for a few seconds, he dipped her low over his arm.

"Axel," she whispered, gazing at him with an inexplicable look in her eyes. They were dark and smoky this evening, teaming with too many emotions to name.

"I really want to kiss you right now."

"We can't," she sighed.

"We can in two and a half more weeks." He reluctantly tugged her upright again.

She gave him a dreamy smile, but didn't answer.

It was all he could do not to capture her lips right then and there to put them both out of their misery. As he led her from the dance floor, they came face to face with Olivia and Edgar Zane.

"My precious boy!" Olivia held out her arms to him and he stepped into them to give her a bear hug. She looked queenly in a formal gown that was a deep shade of purple. Her ebony hair was piled high and secured with crystal pins. A matching crystal choker graced her neck.

Edgar was wearing a black tuxedo with tails and a Regency style top hat. "Introduce us to your lovely guest, son."

"Mom, Dad, this is Kristi Kimiko. Kristi, these are my parents, Olivia and Edgar Zane."

"We are so glad you came this evening." Olivia let go of Axel to air-kiss Kristi's cheek.

Edgar stepped forward to shake her hand. "It's very nice to meet you." He glanced back at Axel. "Did you two get something to eat yet?"

"No." Axel waggled his eyebrows suggestively at Kristi. "Are you hungry?"

"A little." She smiled. "But the food looks almost too pretty to eat."

Olivia looked pleased. "Pretty or not, I'd rather it not go to waste." She beckoned for Kristi to walk with her.

On their way to the food line, the two women walked a few strides ahead of Axel and his father. He overheard them chatting about some garden club where they determined Olivia had met Kristi's grandmother.

"How has Mom been holding up this evening?" He spoke in undertones, not wanting her to hear their conversation.

Edgar Zane pursed his lips. "It's hard, but she's

putting on a good face for Kiera, and Kiera's putting on a good face for her."

"They're pretty special, aren't they?"

"They're my whole world, Axel. You, too."

"Thanks for including me in that."

Marcus's father slapped him on the shoulders. "Thank you for being a part of our family. It's been a lot easier on all of us Zanes since you showed up."

The feeling is mutual. "It's been a lot easier on me, too." Axel could no longer imagine going back to being on his own. He'd always longed for a real family, and he'd finally found one.

"We're stronger together than apart. It's what being a family is all about," Mr. Zane noted matter-of-factly.

"We are." Axel noted. "Speaking of which, I'm glad I could make it to Keira's party, and I'm pretty sure I owe that to you."

"It was mostly Olivia's doing," his father admitted with a twinkle in his eyes. "She can be pretty persuasive."

Axel knew he was only being modest. Both of them had worked hard to make this happen. "You went all out on the food and decorations."

"For obvious reasons."

"Figured that."

"It's a nice girl you invited as your plus one."

"Glad you approve of her."

"That sounds serious." Mr. Zane gave him a searching sideways glance.

"It's the first time I've ever felt this way about someone." It felt good to finally admit it aloud to someone.

"Then it's a good thing she likes you in return."

Axel's heart pounded. "Yeah? How can you tell?"

"The way she looks at you." Edgar Zane nudged his shoulder with his own shoulder in a way that reminded him of Marcus. "It's a lot like the way you look at her."

"I'm falling for her." He was going to ask her on a date the moment he graduated.

"I'm not the one you need to be telling. She is. Have you?"

"In so many words."

"Don't play that game, son. Life is too short." Emotion darkened his father's gaze. He knew what he was talking about.

"I can't do anything about it right now. For a couple more weeks, she's one of my instructors."

"Is that right? What does she teach?"

"Dog handling. Search and rescue stuff."

"You're kidding!" Edgar Zane sounded incredulous. "That tiny little woman?"

"She's terrifying in cargo pants and combat boots."

His father grinned. "She sounds perfect for you."

"I agree. I've already dropped several hints about making her my Mrs. someday."

"You did what?" Mr. Zane threw an arm around Axel's shoulders and drew him aside. "There's supposed to be an order to these things, you know. You date. You tell her you love her. Then you propose."

Axel laughed. "Says who?"

"I do." Edgar Zane arched his brows in amazement.

"I thought everything was fair in love and war."

"Even so, you're going about everything backwards. Trust me."

Axel knowingly wagged a finger in the air. "Point is...she didn't say no."

"By that, I gather she didn't say yes, either."

"But she didn't say no."

They burst out laughing together. It felt good to be joking around with Marcus's dad. It was as if the Lord had decided to restore all the damaged and missing pieces in Axel's life at the same time. He'd gone — almost overnight — from being completely alone in the world to having a real family. Parents, a sister, and a woman he was fairly sure was falling for him as fast as he was falling for her. If he was right, that meant he'd soon be gaining a grandmother, as well.

"It's good to see you happy again." Mr. Zane beamed proudly at him.

"Thank you." For the first time in a long time, the familiar ache of guilt did not accompany his words.

Edgar Zane abruptly changed the subject. "How are those legs healing up?"

"Almost as good as new. I may always have a souvenir limp to remind me of Kandahar, but I can do everything I need to do on them."

"And the PTSD?"

Axel nodded thoughtfully. "Better. A lot better. It's nearly gone." He wasn't quite sure yet if it was the training center wearing him down, or if the change was permanent. "I sleep at night. I get up the next day. I train all day at the Texas Hotline Training Center, and I have no trouble going back to sleep the next night."

"What does the doctor say?"

"Guess I'll find out at the next appointment. In the meantime, I'm enjoying feeling normal again."

Olivia rushed over to them with Kristi on her heels. "Has anyone seen Kiera? It's time to cut the cake, and she's just...gone!"

Alarm speared through Axel. "When was the last time you saw her?"

"I don't know for sure." Olivia pressed a hand to her forehead in agitation. "I remember seeing her dance with you. After that, she danced with her father. Then I think I saw her talking with friends in the food line."

Now would be a good time to have Diesel by my

side. Axel met Kristi's worried gaze and wondered if she was thinking the same thing. "We should probably split up to search the house and yard."

"Good idea." Edger swept off his top hat and ran a hand over his hair. "Probably wouldn't hurt to send someone down to the lakes, as well." The neighborhood where the Zanes lived had several man-made lakes with paved walkways around them.

"I'll do it," Axel offered.

"I'll go with you," Kristi echoed.

They tracked Kiera down by the nearest lake. She was alone in one of the many gazebos dotting the water's edge, sobbing uncontrollably.

Axel jogged up the steps of the gazebo two at a time. "Kiera! What's wrong?" He joined her on the wooden bench and gathered her close.

She buried her face against his chest and cried until his shirt felt damp.

Kristi took a seat on the other side of her and watched them in silence, anxiety etched in her features.

Axel dug his phone from his pocket and handed it to her. "Would you please call Olivia and Edgar, and let them know we found her? I've got them both on speed dial." He didn't care to leave Kiera alone long enough to make the call himself.

"Of course I will." She stepped to the other side of the gazebo to dial the phone.

"I-I s-saw him, Axe!" Kiera finally gasped.

"Saw who?" He stared at her, mystified.

"M-Marcus!"

His hands froze on her shoulders. *Aw, snap!* He'd heard of people going through stuff like this when they were grieving — wanting to see a missing loved one again so badly that they conjured up their face. Basically, it was like hallucinating, and it came as no surprise to Axel that it would happen to Kiera on her birthday. It must be tearing her apart to be forced to celebrate her eighteenth birthday without Marcus.

"We should get you to the doctor," he noted quietly. A car motor droned in the distance and grew louder.

"No!" Kiera slapped her hands against his chest and angrily raised her head. "I'm not crazy!"

He heard the sound of a car door opening and closing. "Of course you're not, baby girl." Olivia materialized at the base of the gazebo steps. Lifting her long skirt, she glided up the stairs to join them.

Edgar was right behind her. "What happened?"

Kiera shot Axel an angry look, daring him to contradict her. "I saw him, Daddy. I saw Marcus. I followed him down the road, and he...disappeared." She shook her head, her eyes filling with a fresh sheen of tears. "I know it sounds crazy. Maybe I *am* crazy."

"Hush, sweet girl." Her mother slid her arms around Kiera's waist and pulled her close. "I don't want to hear any more talk about being crazy. Nobody here is crazy," she added firmly. "You've been through a lot, hon. That's all."

In the end, the Zanes decided to wrap up her birthday celebration early. They ushered their guests home amidst a flood of thank you's for hosting such an amazing get-together.

Shortly afterward, Kristi said her goodbyes to the Zanes and pulled Axel aside in the driveway. "Are you planning on coming back to the training center tonight? I'm asking because I can help you file for an emergency leave of absence if you think you need to stay here."

It was growing dark. A trio of outdoor lanterns enveloped them in a golden glow.

"I'll be back," he assured, drawing her into his embrace, needing to hold her close a few moments to fortify himself against the coming days when he would be unable to do so.

"I need to get going." But she made no move to leave his arms yet.

"I know." He laid his cheek against the top of her head. "I hope you realize I'm going to be fantasizing about having you in my arms again every time I look at you in class."

"Right back atcha, soldier."

He tightened his arms around her. "You're not making this any easier."

"Wasn't trying to."

"Do you have any idea how badly I want to kiss you right now?" he groaned.

"Yes." She reluctantly took a step back. "Two and a half weeks, Axel."

"Yeah, and it's going to feel like two and a half years," he grumbled.

CHAPTER 8: DALLAS DISASTER
KRISTI

Kristi didn't know who was looking forward to Axel's graduation more — her or Axel. He was an incredible student who'd proven to have a clear affinity for training Diesel.

Some handlers worked better than others with their K9 partners, depending on their experience levels and a number of other factors. Even without having a ton of experience working together, Axel and Diesel blended their efforts like salt and pepper. It was the only way Kristi could think to describe their performance during class. They anticipated each other's actions and provided complimentary reactions, often working so closely in tandem on the obstacle courses that they looked like one fluid creature in motion.

Some of the more amateur students made the mistake of being too friendly with their dogs. Not

Axel. He instinctively knew he had to be the alpha in their partnership. She watched Diesel yield time and time again to his handler's commands. She knew it was because the dog trusted his owner implicitly. That, in itself, was a miracle. Not every search and rescue dog could transition so seamlessly to a new handler. Some dogs simply had to be retired at this point in their careers.

The usual percentage of THTC candidates dropped out or failed to meet the requirements for graduation. Out of the seventy-five who'd started their training together, forty-eight proudly assembled in the auditorium on graduation day. Axel was sitting in the same seat in the front row where he'd begun his journey a month earlier. And like he had during the orientation briefings, he sought out and held Kristi's gaze for most of the ceremony.

I love him. Kristi's heart fluttered in her chest at the realization. She knew it was illogical and unlikely to fall for a man that she'd never formally dated, much less kissed. It was an anomaly she might never be able to explain with science or her usual reasoning skills. But the fact remained, she'd somehow fallen in love with Axel Hammerstone.

It was something she was choosing to simply accept.

She was no longer afraid about embarking on a long distance relationship with him after graduation. They would figure it out, and they would make it work. What was happening between them was too strong and too real to vanish once a few miles were between them. Her heart raced in anticipation of the first kiss they would share.

Her toes curled in her combat boots as her mind conjured up a dozen breathtaking scenarios of what it would feel like when he finally claimed his first kiss. Would he steal a quick brush of lips inside one of the training center's hallways? Or would he wait until they reached the parking lot to finish storming and conquering her heart in true Marine style?

The training center's commander took the stage and gave a few opening remarks. Then he launched right into calling the names of the graduates. They marched to the stage one-by-one to accept their diplomas.

"Gunnery Sergeant Axel Smith Hammerstone."

Axel's classmates erupted into applause as their favorite veteran limped his way to the front of the room.

Kristi's heart swelled with pride and adoration as he shot her one of his cocky grins on his way past her.

The female soldier from Iraq got nearly as loud of a response from her classmates. She'd made an amazing contribution to their class, encouraging and helping everyone she could. Colonel Schwarz had written a special commendation for her to take back to her unit, one he hoped would earn her an extra ribbon on her uniform.

As the closing remarks drifted around them like snow, Kristi could hardly contain her excitement. In moments, Axel would no longer be her student. He would be a free man again.

"Class dismissed!" the commander barked for the last time.

The auditorium erupted into loud cheers. Classmates clapped each other on their backs and issued congratulations. Their faces were wreathed in smiles.

Everyone's except Axel's face, that is. From the sideline of the stage, Kristi watched him pull out his cell phone to accept a call. Frowning at whatever was said to him, he abruptly pivoted to stride up the aisle of the auditorium.

Whoever had called him had delivered bad news. Kristi could sense it. So she did the first thing that came to mind. She hurried to the kennel where Diesel was housed. Axel would have to make a stop there to collect his dog before heading anywhere else.

Or so she hoped. Her heart pounded anxiously as two minutes ticked past. Then three. Then five. She gulped and stared at the door. Surely, he wouldn't have left campus without saying goodbye! Would he?

He finally burst into the building. "There you are," he exploded, eyeing her with concern. "I've been looking all over for you."

Her heart shook at the sight of him. "I saw you get a phone call and leave the building, and I was afraid of missing you altogether. I figured this was the one place you—"

"I'm glad you did." Despite the concern darkening his eyes as he strode determinedly in her direction, he was here and he was hers — all hers now. "I didn't want to leave without seeing you."

So, he was leaving town. Her heart pitched with dread at the necessity of him departing so soon. "Why? What's going on?"

His expression darkened another few degrees. "The Dallas-Fort Worth area suffered an earthquake right about the time our graduation ceremony began. If I hadn't had my phone turned off..." He shook his head as he stepped around her to open Diesel's cage. "Come on, boy! Looks like you and I are going back to work right away."

"Right now?" Kristi was aghast. It was his graduation day, for crying out loud! They hadn't had the chance to celebrate it yet. Or to go on their first date. Or share their first kiss.

"I have to, Kristi. The station just called to let me know there are fires raging all over the city, buildings collapsed, people trapped inside..." He shook his head regretfully. "It's what we spent the last month training for. I have to go help."

"Of course you do." She watched him dizzily as he gathered up Diesel's things. This was what it would be like to date a firefighter. She would never know the next time he might be called away from her. She followed him out of the door of the kennel, knowing he had to leave but in no way ready to say goodbye. "I'll go with you." If things were as bad as he said they were, the city was going to need all the help they could get.

He rounded on her. "Dallas is like a war zone right now. It's best to let the first responders do their initial assessments before—"

"What about the Zanes?" Her mind raced feverishly to recall when her grandmother was supposed to be back from her shopping spree with friends in San Antonio. "Have you been able to get in contact with them?"

"Not yet." He shook his head. "I'll keep trying to reach them on the drive up. When was the last time you spoke to your grandmother?"

"Yesterday. She's on a shopping spree with friends in San Antonio." *I think. Please, God! Let her still be out of town!* Gulping back a burst of panic, she dug for her phone and hastily dialed her grandmother. It just kept ringing.

"No answer?" Axel growled.

"No answer." Her voice shook. "I'll go get my keys."

"No!" He stepped in front of her to block her path. "They're shutting the roads down to all incoming traffic other than authorized emergency personnel. It's not safe to be in Dallas right now."

"Axel!" She shoved at his chest. "I am not going to sit here doing nothing for the next several hours, wondering if the only family member I have left in the world is dead or alive. You can't ask that of me."

His hands closed over hers. "That's exactly what I'm asking of you, babe." He ducked his head to scowl directly into her face. "If we're going to be together as a couple, you're going to have to let me do my job in times like these. You're going to have to trust God and pray. Most importantly, you're going to have to stay where it's safe, so you're one less thing I have to worry about."

"But—"

"But nothing!" He scanned her features as if trying to memorize them. "I can't be worried about you and do the things I have to do. You're too important to me."

"Wow!" She was too upset to mask her sarcasm, too close to tears as she teetered on the brink of terror. "You transitioned really quickly from a respectful student to a hard-as-nails, insufferable, overbearing—"

"You want to call me names?" His jaw hardened stubbornly. "Fine. Just don't forget this one. I'm the man who loves you, Kristi Kimiko."

You love me? Time seemed to stand still as she stared at him, utterly stunned. *I mean, I kind of had my suspicions, but hearing it out loud really changes... well, everything.*

He reluctantly twisted away from her to load Diesel into his travel cage. His duffel and backpack were already piled into the backseat. She briefly closed her eyes as the pain of parting washed over her. This wasn't how his graduation day was supposed to have gone. She wasn't near ready to say goodbye. Heaven only knew when she would see him again.

"I'm sorry about having to cut our celebration short, darling." Axel's arms gently came around her. "I'll make it up to you when this is all over, I promise."

Her eyelids flew open. "I know you will. About my grandmother—"

"I'll check on her home and give you a full report. Promise! I'm just glad she's out of town." His mouth came down on hers in a swift but firm kiss that lived up to all of her daydreams except one. It was way too short.

Then he was gone in the roar of a truck engine.

She stared after him, still absorbing the storm of emotions he'd stirred in her. She touched her hand to her lips, reliving every detail of her tumultuous parting from Axel.

I'm the man who loves you. He'd all but shouted the words at her. They'd been close to having their first argument, yet he'd somehow managed to turn even that into something romantic.

I love you, too, Axel. Their whole encounter had been so rushed and had ended so quickly that she was just now realizing she'd not gotten around to saying the words back to him. *I do love you. So much!* She really wished she'd told him. What he did for a living was dangerous. So dangerous that she might not get another chance.

Close to tears, she dialed her grandmother again. Again, there was no response.

"I can't do this," she whispered. *I'm sorry, Axel, but I can't. I don't have it in me to just sit here and wait.* She was an expert search and rescue trainer — not some shrinking, helpless arm-candy girlfriend. And respect traveled in two directions. If she was going to have to accept Axel as the firefighter/EMT that he was, he was going to have to accept her for the SAR professional that she was.

Her mind made up, she raced back to her cabin and threw together a quick overnight bag. Then she grabbed her keys and hopped in her Land Rover at the curb.

Though she had the rest of the weekend off, she sent a quick voice text to Brick Mulligan before she started rolling. *Family emergency. Heading to Dallas.*

The two-and-a-half-hour trip to the city felt like a million years. Kristi continued to dial her grandmother every few minutes without luck. She wanted to call Axel, but she was too afraid he might try to stop her from doing what she was about to do.

Instead, she turned on the radio and listened to each horrifying news update. If she understood the newscaster correctly, her grandmother's townhome was located in the heart of the area that had received the worst brunt of the quake.

Please don't be home, Grandma! Please don't! With each mile she drove, though, her fears grew. Her grandmother had missed phone calls before. Who didn't? Life happened. Baths and showers happened. However, Aimi Kimiko had always called back within minutes. Something was wrong. Kristi could sense it.

A half-mile outside of the Dallas city limits, she ran into the first roadblock. Police officers were turning cars around by having them drive across the median. The grass was starting to get really mashed down in places.

In a frantic bid to buy some time, Kristi flashed her THTC instructor badge at the officer. "Listen, I'm a certified search and rescue instructor and emergency preparedness expert from the Texas Hotline Training Center. I was following firefighter Axel Hammerstone to the station to help out. Our vehicles got separated on the highway."

"Can I see your driver's license, ma'am?"

She produced it, and he hastily scanned it. "What the heck?" he sighed. "We need all the help we can get." He made a rally sign over his head. "Let her through. She's on her way to the firehouse."

The deputy helping him man the checkpoint grabbed one end of the blockade and slid it aside so she could drive past. Elated that she'd actually made it into the city, she waited until she was out of sight of the barricade to switch directions. Instead of heading to the firehouse, she set her course for her grandmother's home. The downed trees, signs, and other carnage made the roads increasingly harder to maneuver. She was forced to park two blocks away in a grocery store parking lot and finish the trip on foot.

When she rounded the final bend in the road, her lips parted in shock to find the entire row of homes billowing with flames. Her grandmother's three-story townhome at the end of the street was the last one standing, though the fire licking across the roof of the nearest building was working its way ever nearer.

Black shingles melted and rolled in rivulets of tar down the sides of the brick. With a great sucking sound, the roof abruptly buckled and collapsed inward. Several burning boards broke loose and filtered to the ground below, making the dry grasses and leaves smoke. Showers of sparks drifted down like orange rain. Then the narrow grassy strip between the two homes erupted in flames. It was only a matter of seconds before they spread to her grandmother's home.

"Grandmother!" Kristi shouted, sprinting down the street. "Grandmother! Where are you?" She spun in a full circle, frantically scanning the faces of the friends and neighbors huddled in the street.

A few shook their heads at her in sympathy.

"Ma'am, stay back," a man shouted. Though she didn't recognize his voice, she could only assume it was a neighbor or a friend of a neighbor. "The fire department is on its way."

She stared at him, aghast. "My grandmother is in there!" she cried. "I have to get her out."

"It's too dangerous," he pleaded. His arms were wrapped around two sobbing girls.

The scream of sirens pierced the air.

"See? They're here," the man's voice turned crooning as he kissed the tops of the girls' heads. "It's going to be alright."

Don't I wish! But Kristi knew better. She wasn't a small child to be soothed. Turning to face her grandmother's home again, she gasped to see the flames climbing up the east wall. She rocked from one foot to the other in agitation. The sirens still sounded too far away, and there was no guarantee they were even coming to this block of homes.

Which meant anyone left in her grandmother's home wouldn't survive.

"I can't," Kristi rasped. Her feet churned into motion. "I'm sorry, but I can't wait."

Ignoring the man as he renewed his shouts of warning, she dashed across the sidewalk and flew up the front porch steps. Producing her key, she stuck it in the door handle and let herself inside. A haze of smoke met her in the entry foyer.

"Grandmother!" she shouted again, waving her hand frenziedly in front of her face. "Are you home?" It was Friday evening. If for any reason she'd come back into town early, she would be home. She never went out on Fridays, claiming she didn't want to get stuck in the crowds of revelers who inevitably flocked to the happy hours taking place all over the city.

Several pieces of furniture were turned on their sides, and broken pottery and crystal littered the floor. Cracks in the drywall streaked their way to the ceiling. It saddened Kristi to see how severely damaged her grandmother's home was from the earthquake. Irreplaceable family photos were lying on their sides beneath spidery splinters of glass.

Holding her arm over her nose and mouth to counter the thickening smoke, Kristi advanced up the stairs to her grandmother's bedroom on the second floor.

"Oh, there you are!" she cried in relief, running into the room and dropping to her knees beside the woman.

Her grandmother was sitting on the floor with her head down, clad in one of her demure house robes speckled with rose buds. She was propped up against the side of her antique four-poster bed.

"We have to get you out of here." Kristi's hands trembled as she reached for the woman's shoulders. Was she hurt? Or even conscious? "There's been an earthquake." She gently shook her shoulders.

"Is that...what happened?" Aimi Kimiko slowly raised her head to meet Kristi's gaze.

"Yes!" Her grandmother was awake. Profound relief flooded her, making her insides weak. "The house next door is on fire, and it's spreading quickly. We need to get out of here. Do you understand what I'm saying?"

Her grandmother nodded. "Then you're going to have to leave me behind, child." Her voice was firm as she tipped her head back against the bed and closed her eyes.

"Why? What happened? You were supposed to be on a shopping trip!" She accused shakily.

"I was tired, so they brought me home early to take a nap. But the shaking started and woke me up. It was so bad that I fell out of bed." Her grandmother gave a sad chuckle. "And now I can't feel my legs."

Kristi's mind raced over the possibilities. It could be a neck or a back injury. Or maybe her grandmother had suffered a stroke, in which case they could be dealing with nerve damage or paralysis.

Generally, it was best not to move the patient under such circumstances until medical help arrived. But they had a fire barreling in their direction. There was no time to wait for help that might never come.

"We have to go," Kristi repeated firmly. "I'll help you." Smoke billowed into the room from the direction of the stairs. "I'll be right back!"

She dashed into the hallway to gauge the source of the smoke and discovered there were flames crawling up the stairs. There was no way she could take her grandmother down them without both of them being roasted alive.

Running back to her grandmother's bedroom, Kristi slammed the door shut. Sprinting to the adjoining bathroom, she yanked a towel off the rack and held it under the faucet until it was soaked. Leaving the water running, she sprinted back to the bedroom and pressed the soggy towel against the opening beneath the door.

She raced to the window next and waved frantically with both hands. "Help," she shouted. "We're trapped!"

At first, those gathered below were too busy pointing and exclaiming over the burning homes to notice her presence. Then a small child caught a glimpse of her and tugged at her mother's hand until the woman glanced up. The woman screamed and pointed at Kristi.

Firemen with ladders converged in her direction.

Hoping it would help, Kristi ran back to the bathroom and soaked more towels. She layered them across the opening of the window. The lower edges of the towels sizzled where the dampness encountered the heat from the ever-climbing flames.

Her grandmother moaned in alarm. "Why is the floor so hot?"

Not good! That had to mean the fire was in the room directly below them. It was only a matter of time before the floor collapsed.

"Come on, grandmother. We have to go. Now!"

Aimi Kimiko pushed at her granddaughter's hands. "I can't, child. You need to—"

"No! I'm not leaving without you, and that's final!" Kristi hooked her arms beneath her grandmother's armpits and slowly dragged her upright. Then she painstakingly walked backwards with her, one step at a time.

The center of the floor made a crackling sound, and the footboard of the four-poster bed canted downward.

"What's happening?" her grandmother babbled, trying to look over her shoulder.

"It's going to be alright," Kristi lied in a crooning voice, holding her grandmother's gaze the same way the man outside had done with his two little girls. "The fire department is here. They're going to get us out." She gritted her teeth as she bumped into something solid. She nearly swooned in relief to realize they'd reached the window.

Hands closed around her shoulders. "Ma'am, if you'll just turn around."

It was a voice she recognized — one she'd been afraid she might never hear again. Unfortunately, smoke and terror clenched her throat, making it impossible to respond. Her arms shook from the effort of holding up her grandmother. *Please, God!* She didn't know how much longer she'd be able to hang on to the precious woman. All she knew was that she wasn't letting go, no matter what.

"Kristi!" Axel shouted hoarsely. "You're alive!" He vaulted into the room beside her.

You came to check on my grandmother! Just like you promised! Tears of gratitude and relief flooded her eyes as he climbed behind her grandmother and slid his arms around their small huddle.

The floor crackled behind them and collapsed. Heat like Kristi had never felt before seared the air around them. It became dizzily apparent that the only reason she and her grandmother hadn't plunged into the fiery inferno below was because Axel was anchoring the three of them against the window sill with his rock-solid arms.

AXEL HELD on with every ounce of strength in him. It was like clinging to the side of the mountain in Kandahar all over again. Fire and smoke surrounded him. Screams and shouts filled his ears. And the heat! It was so unbearable that it was all he could do to contain his own screams.

Please, God! Help me hang on.

It felt like an eternity until a set of gloved hands reached inside the window, then another set. A canvas strap surrounded him and was cinched tightly against his burning skin. There was a dragging sensation and a blast of blessedly cool air.

Then everything went black.

EPILOGUE

Four weeks later

"Axel!" Kristi cried joyfully at the sight of his truck pulling to the curb. She jumped up from her perch on the front porch steps and ran down the sidewalk in his direction. He was supposed to be inside his apartment, convalescing — per doctor's orders — but it looked like he had other things in mind.

It was Friday evening, and she'd come to check on him the moment she got back to Dallas from the Texas Hotline Training Center.

Axel hopped down from behind the wheel and jogged around the side of his truck to catch her in his embrace. He lifted her feet off the ground and gave her a twirl.

"Hello, beautiful!"

"Where did you go?" she chided.

"Out." He grinned down at her before claiming her mouth with his.

The stresses of her week faded beneath the tenderness of his kiss. She clung to him, just grateful to be alive — grateful that all three of them were alive. She and her grandmother had suffered third-degree burns from the fire. Additionally, her grandmother had fractured her hip when she'd fallen out of bed during the earthquake. Axel, on the other hand, was still recovering from second-degree burns on his back and shoulders.

She kept her arms carefully twined around his neck after he lifted his head, not wanting to accidentally bump any of the wounds still healing on his shoulder blades. "You're supposed to be resting and healing, remember?" She anxiously scanned his features, searching for any signs of pain.

"So are you." He ducked his head over hers for another kiss. "Half days, easing back into your work schedule, taking it easy. Does any of that sound familiar to you, Instructor Kimiko?" He walked her backward toward the porch.

She flushed guiltily. There'd simply been too much to do! She and Brick had another group of recruits to train. Though her boss was trying to help out with some of her regular responsibilities, there was only one of him and only so much time in the day in which to get everything done.

"I love you!" She smiled sunnily up at him,

thrilled that she'd been given another chance to say those words. She repeated them as often as possible.

"Nice attempt at distraction, darling, but I asked you a question first."

"I love you so much I can hardly stand it." She tightened her arms around his neck and rested her head against his shoulder. It was true. The way she felt about him was so intense at times that it scared her, but she couldn't help it.

"Better," he muttered against her hairline. "I love you, too. So much that I'll probably never stop having nightmares about how close I came to losing you in the fire." His voice grew rough as he cuddled her closer.

"I'm so sorry for putting you through that, but I had to go after my grandmother."

"I know. She wouldn't have made it out of the house without your help, a fact that will not lessen the severity of my nightmares any time soon."

"We both did our jobs," she said simply, thankful that he was finally able to accept that fact. He may not like the risks she'd taken, but he respected why she'd done it.

"I think you went well above the call of duty, darling. And because of it, you saved a life."

"I couldn't have done it without your help. You know it." She lifted her head to gaze adoringly at him. As usual, he was being modest, but she'd been there. She could attest first hand to the fact that he'd put everything on the line to save them. "You're not just a hero. You're *my* hero."

"I reckon you can thank me with a kiss." Without waiting for her reply, he swooped in to seal his mouth over hers yet again.

Kristi smiled against his lips. They kissed a lot, something she didn't mind one bit. After an entire month of not being able to kiss, they had a lot of lost time to make up for. "Just so you know, Grandmother thinks they should cast you in the lead role of the next blockbuster superhero movie."

He shook his head at her. "She was barely conscious that afternoon. I think the details of what happened have become greatly embellished."

Kristi wrinkled her nose, pretending to consider her words. "Well, maybe the part about the Captain America suit she thought you were wearing is a bit much."

"Like I said..."

"I could probably order you one online, though, and make an honest woman out of her."

He snorted. "Marines don't wear leotards, darling."

"Oh, come on! You'd look great in one."

"Nope. Not happening."

"I could even have a matching one made for Diesel."

"He feels the same way as me about leotards. Trust me."

"At least, run it past him."

"Pass."

She snuggled closer. "Hey, there's something else I've been wanting to tell you."

"Please assure me it doesn't involve me or my dog donning superhero outfits."

"Correct. I finally decided on my answer to that question you asked me during our ambulance ride to the hospital."

He grew still. "Kristi? Are you talking about what I think you're talking about?"

"Yes. If the offer is still on the table, I want to marry you, Axel." *The sooner, the better.* No, dating him from long distance hadn't been easy. Yes, their lives were a little complicated, but she didn't care. She just wanted to be with him, forever and always.

With a whoop of exultation, he scooped her up in his arms and sat down on the front porch steps with her in his lap.

"Of course, the offer is still open." He nuzzled his nose against hers. "You make me happier than I thought was possible."

"I just wanted to be sure," she murmured dreamily. "You were a little delirious when you popped the question."

"Not true. I was in a lot of pain, but I knew exactly what I was saying when I proposed to you."

"Last question. Are you sure you want to be

married to a nerdy gal like me?" It was only fair to lay all of her cards on the table.

"Is the sky blue?"

"I'll drown you with facts and numbers."

"Please do." He grinned at her. "A guy can't have too many of those."

"I'm serious, Axel."

"So am I, babe. Seriously in love with you." He sobered. "Speaking of which, I drove downtown to pick this up for you." He shifted her weight on his lap so he could reach inside the pocket of his jeans. He produced a black velvet box and flipped open the lid for her.

A princess cut diamond set in a white gold band sparkled up at her.

"Axel!" she breathed, her eyes misting with tears. "Oh, Axel!" It was all the proof she needed that he was serious about proposing to her.

"Baby, I was going to keep asking you to marry me until I wore you down." He removed the ring from the box and slid it on her finger. It was a perfect fit.

She held it up so the facets could catch the sun. "I still can't believe how quickly we fell in love. Do you think it's because we weren't allowed to do anything about our feelings for so long?"

"No idea. All I know is that when you showed up as my plus one at Kiera's birthday party, my heart shot well past the point of no return." His chuckle was husky with emotion. "To this day, I don't know how I got through the evening without kissing you."

"It was our ground rules, remember?" A giggle escaped her.

"Maybe. And now it's my turn to lay down a few ground rules." He hitched her closer.

"Mm-hmm?"

"From now on, not a day will go by that I don't tell you I love you, and you tell me how much you love me in return."

"Deal." She trailed a finger down his cheek. "Anything else?"

"If our jobs weren't so far apart, I'd put in a standing order for no less than a dozen kisses from you every day of the week."

"There might actually be a work-around for that."

"Oh?" Hope lit his gaze. "What's that?"

"How do you feel about securing your pilot's license?"

"If it leads to a dozen kisses per day from you, count me in!"

"Good, because that new townhome my grandmother is purchasing has a helipad on the roof."

"You're kidding!"

"She's been shopping for choppers for days with some dealer downtown."

"So if I get my helicopter license, I can come pick

you up for dinner during the week." A grin slowly spread across his face.

"Or you could meet me at the diner."

In reality, it wouldn't be possible for them to be together every evening, but they would be able to see a lot more of each other than they did now.

"I like it," he mused, looking thoughtful. "I think the fire chief will, too. It would allow our search and rescue team to expand our TEXSAR capabilities to mountain rescues."

"That's awesome!" She couldn't resist teasing him some more, though. "Of course, there's the risk the helicopter might come with a superhero outfit for the pilot. It's Grandmother we're talking about here."

"Yeah, that's still not happening." Axel reached up to cup her face. "Since we'll be seeing more of each other, though, we should probably go ahead and add a minimum number of kisses per week to our ground rules."

"As a numbers gal, that sounds right down my alley." She gazed at him with her heart in her eyes.

"Good. Because, as you well know, I'm a firm believer in training. And the way I see it, we have a lifetime of being together to get practiced up for."

"Excellent point, soldier." Her heart sang at the knowledge that he was referring to their wedding. Knowing him, they would be setting a date very soon.

His lips touched hers again, ending all conversation about ground rules. He belonged to her now, and she belonged to him. That was all that mattered.

Like this book? Leave a review!

Then keep turning the page for a sneak peek at
THE SECRET BABY RESCUE

Much love,
Jo

SNEAK PREVIEW: THE SECRET BABY RESCUE

A Marine trying to right an old wrong, a celebrity actress struggling to prove herself in the world of search and rescue operations, and the amber alert that forces them to put everything on the line — including their hearts.

Hunt Ryker's search for a missing Marine comrade lands him in a temporary instructor position at the elite Texas Hotline Training Center. On day one, he meets Dallas Hill, who's tired of not being taken seriously as the lead dog handler at her local search and rescue unit. A former celebrity actress, she impresses him with her all-in attitude toward her new career, as well as her determination to make a difference in the world, one missing child at a time.

When a shocking abduction rocks the town, they

find themselves fighting a sizzling attraction in a race against the clock to bring a mystery child home.

Grab your copy in eBook, paperback, or Kindle Unlimited on Amazon!
The Secret Baby Rescue

Complete series. Read them all!
The Plus One Rescue
The Secret Baby Rescue
The Bridesmaid Rescue
The Girl Next Door Rescue
The Secret Crush Rescue
The Bachelorette Rescue
The Rebound One Rescue
The Fake Bride Rescue
The Blind Date Rescue
The Maid by Mistake Rescue
The Unlucky Bride Rescue
The Temporary Family Rescue

Much love,
Jo

NOTE FROM JO

Guess what? There's more going on in the lives of the hunky heroes you meet in my stories.

Because...*drum roll*...I have some Bonus Content for

everyone who signs up for my mailing list. From now on, there will be a special bonus content for each new book I write, just for my subscribers. Also, you'll hear about my next new book as soon as it's out (*plus you get a free book in the meantime*). Woohoo!

As always, thank you for reading and loving my books!

JOIN CUPPA JO READERS!

If you're on Facebook, please join my group, Cuppa Jo Readers. Don't miss out on the giveaways + all the sweet and swoony cowboys!

https://www.facebook.com/groups/CuppaJoReaders

FREE BOOK!

Don't forget to join my mailing list for new releases, freebies, special discounts, and Bonus Content. Plus, you get a FREE sweet romance book for signing up!

https://BookHip.com/JNNHTK

SNEAK PREVIEW: ACCIDENTAL HERO

Matt Romero was single again, and this time he planned to stay that way.

Feeling like the world's biggest fool, he gripped the steering wheel of his white Ford F-150, cruising up the sunny interstate toward Amarillo. He had an interview in the morning, so he was arriving a day early to get the lay of the land. That, and he was anxious to put as many miles as possible between him and his ex.

It was one thing to have allowed himself to become blinded by love. It was another thing entirely to have fallen for the stupidest line in a cheater's handbook.

Cat sitting. I actually allowed her to talk me into cat sitting! Plus, he'd collected his fiancée's mail and carried her latest batch of Amazon deliveries into her condo.

It wasn't that he minded helping out the woman he planned to spend the rest of his life with. What he minded was that she wasn't in New York City on business like she'd claimed. *Nope.* As it turned out, she was nowhere near the Big Apple. It had simply been her cover story for cheating on him, the first lie in a long series of lies.

To make matters worse, she'd recently talked Matt into leaving the Army for her, a decision he'd probably regret for the rest of his life now that she'd broken their engagement and moved on with someone else.

Leaving me single, jobless, and —

The scream of sirens jolted Matt back to the present. A glance in his rearview mirror confirmed his suspicions. He was getting pulled over. *For what?* A scowl down at his speedometer revealed he was cruising at no less than 95 mph. *Whoa!* It was a good twenty miles over the posted speed limit. *Okay, this is bad.* He'd be lucky if he didn't lose his license over this — his fault entirely for driving distracted without his cruise control on. *My day just keeps getting better.*

Slowing and pulling his truck over to the shoulder, he coasted to a stop and waited. And waited. And waited some more. A peek in his side mirror showed the cop was still sitting in his car and talking on his phone.

Oh, come on! Just give me my ticket already.

To stop the pounding between his temples, Matt reached for the red cooler he'd propped on the passenger seat and pulled out a can of soda. He popped the tab and tipped it up to chug down a shot of caffeine. He hadn't slept much the last couple of nights.

Before he could take a second sip, movement in the rearview mirror caught his attention. He watched as the police officer finally opened his door, unfolded his large frame from the front seat of his black SUV, and stood. However, he continued talking on his phone instead of walking Matt's way.

Are you kidding me? Matt swallowed a dry chuckle and took another swig of his soda. It was a good thing he'd hit the road the day before his interview at the Pantex nuclear plant. At the rate his day was going, it might take the rest of the afternoon to collect his speeding ticket.

He'd reached the outskirts of Amarillo, only about twenty to thirty miles from his final destination. The exit sign for Hereford was up ahead. Or the Beef Capital of the World, as the small farm town was often called.

He reached across the dashboard to open his glove compartment and fish out his registration card and proof of insurance. His gut told him there wasn't going to be any talking his way out of this one. As a general rule, men in blue didn't sympathize with folks going twenty miles or more over the speed limit.

Digging for his wallet, he pulled out his driver's license. Out of sheer habit, he reached inside the slot where he normally kept his military ID and found it empty. *Right.* He no longer possessed one, which left him with an oddly empty feeling.

He took another gulp of soda and watched as the officer pocketed his cell phone. *Finally! Guess that means it's time to get this party started.* Matt chunked his soda can into the nearest cup holder and stuck his driver's license, truck registration, and insurance card between two fingers. Hitting an automatic button on the door, he lowered his window a few inches and waited.

The guy strode up to Matt's truck window with a bit of a swagger. His tan Stetson was pulled low over his eyes. "License and registration, soldier."

Guess you noticed the Ranger tab on my license plate. Matt wordlessly poked the requested items through the window opening.

"Any reason you're in such a hurry this morning?" the officer mused curiously as he scanned Matt's identification. He was so tall, he had to stoop to peer through the window. Like Matt, he had a dark tan, brown hair, and a goatee. The two of them could've passed as cousins or something.

"Nothing worth hearing, officer." *My problem. Not yours. Don't want to talk about it.* Matt squinted through the glaring sun to read the guy's name on his tag. *McCarty.*

"That's too bad, because I always have plenty of time to chat when I'm writing up such a hefty ticket." Officer McCarty's tone was mildly sympathetic, though it was impossible to read his expression behind his sunglasses. "I clocked you going twenty-two miles over the posted limit, Mr. Romero."

Twenty-two miles? Yeah, that's not good. Not good at all. Matt's jaw tightened, and he could feel the veins in his temples throbbing. It looked like he was going to have to share his story, after all. Maybe, just maybe, the trooper would feel so sorry for him that he'd give him a warning instead of a ticket. It was worth a try, anyway. *If nothing else, it'll give you something to laugh about during your next coffee break.*

"Today was supposed to be my wedding day." He spoke through stiff lips, finding a strange sort of relief in confessing that sorry fact to a perfect stranger. Fortunately, they'd never have to see each other again.

"I'm sorry for your loss." Officer McCarty glanced up from Matt's license to give him what felt like a piercing once over. He was probably trying to gauge if he was telling the truth or not.

"Oh, she's still alive," Matt muttered. "Found somebody else, that's all." He gripped the steering wheel and drummed his thumbs against it. *I'm just the poor fool she cheated on.*

He was so done with dating. At the moment, he

couldn't imagine ever again putting his heart on the chopping block of love. *Better to be lonely than to let another person destroy you like that.* She'd taken everything from him that mattered — his pride, his dignity, even his career.

"Ouch," Officer McCarty sighed. "Well, here comes the tough part about my job. Despite your reasons for speeding, you were putting lives at risk. Your own included."

"Can't disagree with that." Matt stared straight ahead, past the small spidery nick in his windshield. He'd gotten hit by a rock earlier while passing a semi tractor trailer. It really hadn't been his day. Or his week. Or his year, for that matter. It didn't mean he was going to grovel, though. He'd tried to appeal to the guy's sympathy and failed. The sooner he gave him his ticket, the sooner they could both be on their way.

A massive dump truck on the oncoming side of the highway abruptly swerved into the narrow, grassy median. It was a few hundred yards away, but the front left tire dipped down, *way* down, making the truck pitch heavily to one side.

"Whoa!" Matt shouted, pointing to get Officer McCarty's attention. "That guy looks like he's in trouble!"

Two vehicles on Matt's side of the road passed him in quick succession — a rusty blue van pulling a fifth wheel and a shiny red Dodge Ram.

When Officer McCarty didn't respond, Matt laid on his horn to warn the two drivers, just as the dump truck started to roll. It was like watching a horror movie in slow motion, knowing something bad was about to happen while being helpless to stop it.

The dump truck slammed onto its side and skidded noisily across Matt's lane. The blue van whipped to the right shoulder in a vain attempt to avoid the collision. Matt winced as the van's bumper caught the hood of the skidding dump truck nearly head on, then jack-knifed into the air.

The driver of the red truck was only a few car lengths behind, jamming so hard on its brakes that it left two dark smoking lines of rubber on the pavement. Seconds later, it careened into the median and flipped on its side. It wasn't immediately clear if the red pickup had collided with any part of the dump truck. However, an ominous swirl of smoke seeped from beneath its hood.

For a split second, Matt and Officer McCarty stared in shock at each other. Then the officer shoved Matt's license and registration back through the opening in the window. "Looks like I've got more important things to do than give you a ticket." He sprinted toward his SUV, leaped inside, and gunned it toward the scene of the accident with his lights flashing and sirens blaring. He only drove a short distance before stopping his vehicle and canting it across both lanes to form a makeshift blockade.

Though Matt was no longer in the military, his defend-and-protect instincts kicked in. There was no telling how long it would take the emergency vehicles to arrive, and he didn't like the way the red pickup was smoking. The driver hadn't climbed out of the cab yet, either, which wasn't a good sign.

Officer McCarty reached the blue van first, probably because it was the closest, and assisted a dazed man from one of the back passenger seats. He led him to the side of the road, helped him get seated on a small incline, then jogged back to help the driver exit the van. Unfortunately, the officer was only one man, and this was much bigger than a one-man job.

Following his gut instincts, Matt disengaged his emergency brake and gunned his way up the shoulder, pausing beside the officer's vehicle. Turning off his motor, he leaped from his truck and jogged across the highway to the red pickup. The motor was still running, and the smoke was rising more thickly now.

Whoever was behind the wheel needed to get out immediately before the thing caught fire or exploded. Matt took a flying leap to hop on top of the cab and crawl to the driver's door. It was locked.

Pounding on the window, he shouted at the driver, "You okay in there?"

There was no answer and no movement. Peering closer, he could make out the unmoving figure of a woman. Blonde, pale, and curled to one side. The only thing holding her in place was the strap of a seatbelt around her waist. A trickle of red ran across one cheek.

Matt's survival training kicked in. Crouching over the side of the truck, he quickly assessed the undamaged windshield and decided it wasn't the best entry point. *Too bad.* Because his only other option was to shower the driver with glass. *Sorry, lady!* Swinging a leg, he jabbed the heel of his boot into the section of window nearest the lock. By some miracle, he managed to pop a fist-sized hole instead of shattering the entire pane.

Reaching inside, he unlocked the door and pulled it open. The next part was a little trickier, since he had to reach down, *way* down, to unbuckle the woman and catch her weight before she fell. It would've been easier if she were conscious and able to follow his instructions.

Guess I'll have to do it without any help. An ominous hiss of steam and smoke from beneath the hood stiffened his resolve and made him move faster.

"Come on, lady," he muttered, releasing her seatbelt and catching her slender frame before she fell. With a grunt of exertion, he hefted her free of the mangled cab. Then he half-slid, half hopped back to the ground with her in his arms. As soon as his boots hit the pavement, he took off at a jog.

She was lighter than he'd been expecting. Her upper arm, that his left hand was cupped around, felt desperately thin despite her baggy pink and plaid shirt. One long, strawberry blonde braid dangled over her shoulder, and a sprinkle of freckles stood out in stark relief against her pale cheeks.

She didn't so much as twitch as he ran with her, telling him that she was still out cold. He hoped it didn't mean she'd hit her head too hard on impact. Visions of traumatic brain injuries and their long list of complications swarmed through his mind, along with the possibility that he might've just finished moving a woman with a broken neck or back. *Please don't let that be the case, Lord.*

He carried her to the far right shoulder and up a grassy knoll where Officer McCarty was depositing the other injured victims. A dry wind gusted, sending a layer of fine dust in their direction. One prickly, rolling tumbleweed followed. On the other side of the knoll was a rocky canyon wall that went straight up, underscoring the fact that there really hadn't been any way for the hapless van and pickup drivers to avoid the collision. They'd literally been trapped between the canyon and oncoming traffic.

An explosion ricocheted through the air, shaking the ground beneath Matt's feet. On pure instinct, he dove for the grass, using his body to shield the woman in his arms. He used one hand to cradle her head against his chest and his other hand to break their fall as best he could.

A few of the other injured drivers and passengers cried out in fear as smoke billowed around them and blanketed the scene. For the next few minutes, it was difficult to see much, though the wave of ensuing heat had a suffocating feel to it. The woman beneath Matt remained motionless, though he thought he heard her mumble something at one point. He continued to crouch over her, keeping her head cradled beneath his hand. He rubbed his thumb beneath her nose and determined she was still breathing. However, she remained unconscious. He debated what to do next.

A fire engine howled in the distance, making his shoulders slump in relief. Help had finally arrived. More sirens blared, and the area was soon crawling with fire engines, ambulances, and paramedics with stretchers. One walked determinedly in his direction.

"Hi! My name is Star, and I'm here to help you. What's your name, sir?" the EMT worker inquired in a calm, even tone. Her chin-length dark hair was blowing nearly sideways in the wind. She shook her head to knock it away, revealing a pair of snapping dark eyes swimming with concern.

"I'm Sergeant Matt Romero," he informed her out of sheer habit. *Well, maybe no longer the sergeant part.* "Don't worry about me. I'm fine. This woman is not. I don't know her name. She was unconscious when I pulled her out of her truck."

As the curvy EMT stepped closer, Matt could read her name tag. *Corrigan.* "Like I said, I'm here to do everything I can to help." Her forehead wrinkled in alarm as she caught sight of the injured woman's face. "Bree?" Tossing her red medical bag on the ground, she slid to her knees beside the two of them. "Oh, Bree, honey!" she sighed, reaching for her pulse.

"I-I..." The woman stirred. Her lashes fluttered a few times against her cheeks. Then they snapped open, revealing two pools of the deepest blue Matt had ever seen. Though glazed with pain, her gaze latched anxiously onto him. "Don't leave me," she pleaded with a hitch in her voice.

There was something oddly personal about the request. Though he was sure they'd never met before, she spoke as if she recognized him. Her confusion tugged at every one of his heartstrings, making him long to grant her request.

"I won't," he promised huskily, hardly knowing what he was saying. In that moment, he probably would have said anything to make the desperate look in her eyes go away.

"I'm not liking her heart rate." Star produced a penlight and flipped it on. Shining it in one of her friend's eyes, then the other, she cried urgently, "Bree? It's me, Star. Can you tell me what happened, hon?"

A shiver worked its way through Bree's too-thin frame. "Don't leave me," she whispered again to Matt, before her eyelids fluttered closed. Another shiver worked its way through her, despite the fact that she was no longer conscious.

"She's going into shock." Star glanced worriedly over her shoulder. "Need a stretcher over here," she called sharply. One was swiftly rolled their way.

Matt helped the EMT lift and deposit their precious burden on it.

"Can you make it to the hospital?" Star asked as he helped push the stretcher toward the nearest ambulance. "Bree seemed pretty insistent about you sticking around."

Matt's eyebrows shot upward in surprise. He hadn't been expecting yet another person he'd never met before to ask him to stick around. "Uh, sure." In her delirium, the injured woman had probably mistaken him for someone else. However, he didn't mind helping out. *Who knows?* Maybe he could give the attending physician some information about her rescue that might prove useful in her treatment.

Or maybe he was just drawn to the fragile-looking Bree for reasons he couldn't explain. Whatever the case, Matt suddenly wasn't feeling in a terrible hurry to hit the road again. Fortunately, he had plenty of extra time built into his schedule before his interview tomorrow. The only real task he had left for the day was finding a hotel room once he reached Amarillo.

"I just need to let Officer McCarty know I'm leaving the scene of the accident." Matt shook his head sheepishly. "I kinda hate to admit this, but he had me pulled over for speeding before everything went down here." He waved a hand at the carnage around them. It was a dismal scene, punctuated by twisted metal and scorched pavement. All three mangled vehicles looked like they were totaled.

Star snickered, then seemed to catch herself. "Sorry. That was inappropriate laughter. Very inappropriate laughter."

He shrugged, not the least bit offended. A lot of people laughed when they were nervous or upset, which Star clearly had been since the moment she'd discovered the unconscious woman was a friend. "It was pretty stupid of me to be driving these long, empty stretches of highway without my cruise control on." Especially with the way he'd been brooding non-stop for the past seventy-two hours.

Star shot him a sympathetic look. "Believe me, I'm not judging. Far from it." She reached out to pat Officer McCarty's arm as they passed by him with the stretcher. "The only reason a bunch of us in Hereford don't have a lot more points on our licenses is because we grew up with this sweet guy."

"Oh, no! Is that Bree?" Officer McCarty groaned. He pulled his sunglasses down to take a closer look over the top of his lenses. His stoic expression was gone. In its place was one etched with worry. The personal kind. Like Star, he knew the victim.

"Yeah." Star's pink glossy lips twisted. "She and her brother can't catch a break, can they?"

Since two more paramedics converged on them to help lift Bree's stretcher into the ambulance, Matt paused to face the trooper who'd pulled him over.

"Any issues with me following them to the hospital, officer? Star asked me if I would." Unfortunately, it would give the guy more time and opportunity to ticket Matt, but that couldn't be helped.

"Emmitt," Officer McCarty corrected. "The name is Emmitt, alright? I think you more than worked off your ticket back there."

Sucking in a breath of relief, Matt held out a hand. "Thanks, man. I really appreciate it." It was a huge concession. The guy could've taken his license if he'd wanted to.

They soberly shook hands, eyeing each other.

"You need me to come by the PD to file a witness report or anything before I boogie out of town this evening?" Matt pressed.

"Nah. Just give me a call, and we'll take care of it over the phone." Emmitt produced a business card and handed it over. "Not sure if we'll need your story, since I saw it go down, but we should probably still cross every T."

"Roger that." Matt stuffed the card in the back pocket of his jeans.

"Where are you headed, anyway?"

"Amarillo. Got an interview at Pantex tomorrow."

"Nice! It's a solid company." Emmitt nodded. "I've got several friends who work there."

Star leaned out from the back of the ambulance. "You coming or what?" she called impatiently to Matt.

He nodded vigorously. "I'll follow you," he called back and jogged back to his truck. Since the ambulance was on the opposite side of the highway, he turned on his blinker and put his oversized tires to good use while traversing the median. He had to spin his wheels a bit in the center of the median to get his tires to grab the sandy incline leading to the other side. He was grateful all over again that he'd splurged on a few upgrades for his truck to make it fit for off-roading.

He followed the ambulance north and found himself driving the final twenty minutes or so to Amarillo, probably because it boasted a much bigger hospital than any of the smaller surrounding towns — more than one, actually. Due to another vehicle leaving the parking lot as he was entering it, Matt was able to grab a decently close parking spot. He jogged into the waiting room, dropped Star Corrigan's name a few times, and tried to make it sound like he was a close friend of the patient.

Looking doubtful, the receptionist made him wait while she paged Star, who appeared a short time later to escort him into the emergency room. "Bree's in Bay 6," she informed him in a strained voice, reaching for his arm and practically dragging him behind the curtain.

If anything, Bree looked even thinner and more fragile than she had outside on the highway. A nurse was stooped over her, inserting an I.V. into her arm.

"She still hasn't woken up." Star's voice was soft, barely above a whisper. "They're pretty sure she has a concussion. Sounds like they're gonna run a full battery of tests to figure out what's going on."

Matt nodded, not knowing what to say.

The lovely EMT's pager went off. She snatched it up and scowled at it. "I just got another call. It's a busy day out there for motorists." She texted a message on her cell phone, then cast him a sideways glance. "Any chance you'll be able to stick around until Bree's brother gets here?"

That's when it hit Matt that this had been the EMT's real goal all along — to ensure that her friend wasn't left alone. She'd known she could get called away to the next job at any second.

"Not a problem." He offered what he hoped was a reassuring smile. Amarillo was where he'd been heading, so he'd already reached his final destination. "I wasn't planning on going far, anyway. Got an interview at Pantex in the morning."

"No kidding! Well, good luck with that," she

returned with a curious, searching look. "A lot of my friends moved up this way for jobs after high school."

Officer Emmitt McCarty had said something similar. "Hey, ah..." Matt hated detaining the EMT any longer than necessary, but it might not hurt to know a few more details about the unconscious woman, since he was about to be alone with her. "Mind telling me Bree's last name?"

"Anderson. Her brother is Brody. Brody Anderson. They run a ranch about halfway between here and Hereford, so it'll take him a good twenty to thirty minutes to get here."

"It's alright. I can stay. It was nice meeting you, by the way." His gaze landed on Bree's left hand, which was resting limply atop the white blankets on her bed. She wasn't wearing a wedding ring. *Not that it matters. I'm a complete idiot for looking.* He forced his gaze back to the EMT. "Sorry about the circumstances, of course."

"Me, too." She shot another worried look at her friend and dropped her voice conspiratorially. "Hey, you're really not supposed to be back here since you're not family, but I sorta begged and they sorta agreed to overlook the rules until Brody gets here." She eyed him worriedly.

"Don't worry." He could tell she hated the necessity of leaving. "I'll stick around until her brother gets here, even if I get booted out to the waiting room with the regular Joes."

"Thanks! Really." She whipped out her cell phone. "Here's my number in case you need to reach me for anything."

Wow! Matt had not been expecting the beautiful EMT to offer him her phone number. Not that he was complaining. It was a boost to his sorely damaged ego. He dug for his phone. "I'm ready when you're ready."

She rattled off her number, and he quickly texted her back so she would have his.

"Take care of her for me, will you, Matt?" she pleaded anxiously.

On second thought, there was nothing flirtatious about Star's demeanor. It was entirely possible that their exchange of phone numbers was exactly what she'd claimed it was — a means of staying in touch about the status of her friend's condition. Giving her a reassuring look, Matt fist-bumped her.

Looking grateful, she pushed aside the curtain and was gone. The nurse followed, presumably to report Bree's vitals to the doctor on duty.

Matt moved to the foot of the hospital bed. "So, who do you think I am, Bree?" *And why did you beg me not to leave you?*

Her long blonde lashes remained motionless against her cheeks. It looked like he was going to have to stick around for a while if he wanted answers.

Accidental Hero
It's available in eBook and paperback on Amazon + FREE in Kindle Unlimited!

Read them all!
A - Accidental Hero
B - Best Friend Hero
C - Celebrity Hero
D - Damaged Hero
E - Enemies to Hero
F - Forbidden Hero
G - Guardian Hero
H - Hunk and Hero
I - Instantly Her Hero
J - Jilted Hero
K - Kissable Hero
L - Long Distance Hero
M- Mistaken Hero
N - Not Good Enough Hero
O - Opposites Attract Hero

Much love,
Jo

SNEAK PREVIEW: HER BILLIONAIRE BOSS

Jacey Maddox didn't bother straightening her navy pencil skirt or smoothing her hand over the sleek lines of her creamy silk blouse. She already knew she looked her best. She knew her makeup was flawless, each dash of color accentuating her sun kissed skin and classical features. She knew this, because she'd spent way too many of her twenty-five years facing the paparazzi; and after her trust fund had run dry, posing for an occasional glossy centerfold — something she wasn't entirely proud of.

Unfortunately, not one drop of that experience lent her any confidence as she mounted the cold, marble stairs of Genesis & Sons. It towered more than twenty stories over the Alaskan Gulf waters, a stalwart high-rise of white and gray stone with tinted windows, a fortress that housed one of the world's most brilliant think tanks. For generations, the sons of Genesis had ridden the cutting edge of industrial design, developing the concepts behind some of the nation's most profitable inventions, products, and manufacturing processes.

It was the one place on earth she was least welcome.

Not just because of how many of her escapades had hit the presses during her rebel teen years. Not just because she'd possessed the audacity to marry their youngest son against their wishes. Not just because she had encouraged him to pursue his dreams instead of their hallowed corporate mission — a decision that had ultimately gotten him killed. No. The biggest reason Genesis & Sons hated her was because of her last name. The one piece of herself she'd refused to give up when she'd married Easton Calcagni.

Maddox.

The name might as well have been stamped across her forehead like the mark of the beast, as she moved into the crosshairs of their first security camera. It flashed an intermittent red warning light and gave a low electronic whirring sound as it swiveled to direct its lens on her.

Her palms grew damp and her breathing quickened as she stepped into the entry foyer of her family's greatest corporate rival.

Recessed mahogany panels lined the walls above a mosaic tiled floor, and an intricately carved booth anchored the center of the room. A woman with silver hair waving past her shoulders lowered her reading glasses to dangle from a pearlized chain. "May I help you?"

Jacey's heartbeat stuttered and resumed at a much faster pace. The woman was no ordinary receptionist. Her arresting blue gaze and porcelain features had graced the tabloids for years. She was Waverly, matriarch of the Calcagni family, grandmother to the three surviving Calcagni brothers. She was the one who'd voiced the greatest protests to Easton's elopement. She'd also wept in silence throughout his interment into the family mausoleum, while Jacey had stood at the edge of their gathering, dry-eyed and numb of soul behind a lacy veil.

The funeral had taken place exactly two months earlier.

"I have a one o'clock appointment with Mr. Luca Calcagni."

Waverly's gaze narrowed to twin icy points. "Not just any appointment, Ms. Maddox. You are here for an interview, I believe?"

Time to don her boxing gloves. "Yes." She could feel the veins pulsing through her temples now. She'd prepared for a rigorous cross-examination but had not expected it to begin in the entry foyer.

"Why are you really here?"

Five simple words, yet they carried the force of a full frontal attack. Beneath the myriad of accusations shooting from Waverly's eyes, she wanted to spin on her peep-toe stiletto pumps and run. Instead, she focused on regulating her breathing. It was a fair question. Her late husband's laughing face swam before her, both taunting and encouraging, as her mind ran over all the responses she'd rehearsed. None of them seemed adequate.

"I'm here because of Easton." It was the truth stripped of every excuse. She was here to atone for her debt to the family she'd wronged.

Pain lanced through the aging woman's gaze, twisting her fine-boned features with lines. Raw fury followed. "Do you want something from us, Ms. Maddox?" Condescension infused her drawling alto.

Not what you're thinking, that's for sure. I'm no gold-digger. "Yes. Very much. I want a job at Genesis." She could never restore Easton to his family, but she would offer herself in his place. She would spend the rest of her career serving their company in whatever capacity they would permit. It was the penance she'd chosen for herself.

The muscles around Waverly's mouth tightened a few degrees more. "Why not return to DRAW Corporation? To your own family?"

She refused to drop the elder woman's gaze as she absorbed each question, knowing they were shot like bullets to shatter her resolve, to remind her how unwelcome her presence was. She'd expected no other reception from the Calcagni dynasty; some would even argue she deserved this woman's scorn. However, she'd never been easily intimidated, a trait that was at times a strength and other times a curse. "With all due respect, Mrs. Calcagni, this *is* my family now."

Waverly's lips parted as if she would protest. Something akin to fear joined the choleric emotions churning across her countenance. She clamped her lips together, while her chest rose and fell several times. "You may take a seat now." She waved a heavily be-ringed hand to indicate the lounge area to her right. Lips pursed the skin around her mouth into papery creases, as she punched a few buttons on the call panel. "Ms. Maddox has arrived." Her frigid tone transformed each word into ice picks.

Jacey expelled the two painful clumps of air her lungs had been holding prisoner in a silent, drawn-out whoosh as she eased past the reception booth. She'd survived the first round of interrogations, a small triumph that yielded her no satisfaction. She knew the worst was yet to come. Waverly Calcagni was no more than a guard dog; Luca Calcagni was the one they sent into the boxing ring to finish off their opponents.

Luca apparently saw fit to allow her to marinate in her uneasiness past their appointment time. Not a surprise. He had the upper hand today and would do everything in his power to squash her with it. A full hour cranked away on the complicated maze of copper gears and chains on the wall. There was nothing ordinary about the interior of Genesis & Sons. Even their clocks were remarkable feats of architecture.

"Ms. Maddox? Mr. Calcagni is ready to see you."

She had to remind herself to breathe as she stood. At first she could see nothing but Luca's tall silhouette in the shadowed archway leading to the inner sanctum of Genesis & Sons. Then he took a step forward into a beam of sunlight and beckoned her to follow him. She stopped breathing again but somehow forced her feet to move in his direction.

He was everything she remembered and more from their few brief encounters. Much more. Up close, he seemed taller, broader, infinitely more intimidating, and so wickedly gorgeous it made her dizzy. That her parents had labeled him and his brothers as forbidden fruit made them all the more appealing to her during her teen years. It took her fascinated brain less than five seconds to recognize Luca had lost none of his allure.

The blue-black sheen of his hair, clipped short on the sides and longer on top, lent a deceptive innocence that didn't fool her one bit. Nor did the errant lock slipping to his forehead on one side. The expensive weave of his suit and complex twists of his tie far better illustrated his famed unpredictable temperament. His movements were controlled but fluid, bringing to her mind the restless prowl of a panther as she followed him down the hall and into an elevator. It shimmered with mirrored glass and recessed mahogany panels.

They rode in tense silence to the top floor.

Arrogance rolled off him from his crisply pressed white shirt, to his winking diamond and white gold cuff links, down to his designer leather shoes. In some ways, his arrogance was understandable. He guided the helm of one of the world's most profitable companies, after all. And his eyes! They were as beautiful and dangerous as the rest of him. Tawny with flecks of gold, they regarded her with open contempt as he ushered her from the elevator.

They entered a room surrounded by glass. One wall of windows overlooked the gulf waters. The other three framed varying angles of the Anchorage skyline. Gone was the old-world elegance of the first floor. This room was all Luca. A statement of power in chrome and glass. Sheer contemporary minimalism with no frills.

"Have a seat." It was an order, not an offer. A call to battle.

It was a battle she planned to win. She didn't want to consider the alternative — slinking back to her humble apartment in defeat.

He flicked one darkly tanned hand at the pair of Chinese Chippendale chairs resting before his expansive chrome desk. The chairs were stained black like the heart of their owner. No cushions.

They were not designed for comfort, only as a place to park guests whom the CEO did not intend to linger.

She planned to change his mind on that subject before her allotted hour was up. "Thank you." Without hesitation, she took the chair on the right, making no pretense of being in the driver's seat. This was his domain. Given the chance, she planned to mold herself into the indispensable right hand to whoever in the firm he was willing to assign her. On paper, she might not look like she had much to offer, but there was a whole pack of demons driving her. An asset he wouldn't hesitate to exploit once he recognized their unique value. Or so she hoped.

To her surprise, he didn't seat himself behind his executive throne. Instead, he positioned himself between her and his desk, hiking one hip on the edge and folding his arms. It was a deliberate invasion of her personal space with all six feet two of his darkly arresting half-Hispanic features and commanding presence.

Most women would have swooned.

Jacey wasn't most women. She refused to give him the satisfaction of either fidgeting or being the first to break the silence. Silence was a powerful weapon, something she'd learned at the knees of her parents. Prepared to use whatever it took to get what she'd come for, she allowed it to stretch well past the point of politeness.

Luca finally unfolded his arms and reached for the file sitting on the edge of his desk. "I read your application and resume. It didn't take long."

According to her mental tally, the first point belonged to her. She nodded to acknowledge his insult and await the next.

He dangled her file above the trash canister beside his desk and released it. It dropped and settled with a papery flutter.

"I fail to see how singing in nightclubs the past five years qualifies you for any position at Genesis & Sons."

The attack was so predictable she wanted to smile, but didn't dare. Too much was at stake. She'd made the mistake of taunting him with a smile once before. Nine years earlier. Hopefully, he'd long forgotten the ill-advised lark.

Or not. His golden gaze fixed itself with such intensity on her mouth that her insides quaked with uneasiness. Nine years later, he'd become harder and exponentially more ruthless. She'd be wise to remember it.

"Singing is one of art's most beautiful forms," she countered softly. "According to recent studies, scientists believe it releases endorphins and oxytocin while reducing cortisol." *There.* He wasn't the only one who'd been raised in a tank swimming with intellectual minds.

The tightening of his jaw was the only indication

her answer had caught him by surprise. Luca was a man of facts and numbers. Her answer couldn't have possibly displeased him, yet his upper lip curled. "If you came to sing for me, Ms. Maddox, I'm all ears."

The smile burgeoning inside her mouth vanished. Every note of music in her had died with her husband. That part of her life was over. "We both know I did not submit my employment application in the hopes of landing a singing audition." She started to rise, a calculated risk. "If you don't have any interest in conducting the interview you agreed to, I'll just excuse my—"

"Have a seat, Ms. Maddox." Her veiled suggestion of his inability to keep his word clearly stung.

She sat.

"Remind me what other qualifications you disclosed on your application. There were so few, they seem to have slipped my mind."

Nothing slipped his mind. She would bet all the money she no longer possessed on it. "A little forgetfulness is understandable, Mr. Calcagni. You're a very busy man."

Her dig hit home. This time the clench of his jaw was more perceptible.

Now that she had his full attention, she plunged on. "My strengths are in behind-the-scenes marketing as well as personal presentations. As you are well aware, I cut my teeth on DRAW Corporation's drafting tables. I'm proficient in an exhaustive list of software programs and a whiz at compiling slides, notes, memes, video clips, animated graphics, and most types of printed materials. My family just this morning offered to return me to my former position in marketing."

"Why would they do that?"

"They hoped to crown me Vice President of Communications in the next year or two. I believe their exact words were *it's my rightful place.*" As much as she tried to mask it, a hint of derision crept in her voice. There were plenty of employees on her family's staff who were far more qualified and deserving of the promotion.

His lynx eyes narrowed to slits. "You speak in the past tense, Ms. Maddox. After recalling what a flight risk you are, I presume your family withdrew their offer?"

It was a slap at her elopement with his brother. She'd figured he'd work his way around to it, eventually. "No." She deliberately bit her lower lip, testing him with another ploy that rarely failed in her dealings with men. "I turned them down."

His gaze locked on her mouth once more. Male interest flashed across his face and was gone. "Why?"

He was primed for the kill. She spread her hands and went for the money shot. "To throw myself at your complete mercy, Mr. Calcagni." The beauty of it was that the trembling in her voice wasn't faked; the request she was about to make was utterly genuine. "As your sister by marriage, I am not here to debate my qualifications or lack of them. I am begging you to give me a job. I need the income. I need to be busy. I'll take whatever position you are willing to offer so long as it allows me to come to work in this particular building." She whipped her face aside, no longer able to meet his gaze. "Here," she reiterated fiercely. "Where *he* doesn't feel as far away as he does outside these walls."

Because of the number of moments it took to compose herself, she missed his initial reaction to her words. When she tipped her face up to his once more, his expression was unreadable.

"Assuming everything you say is true, Ms. Maddox, and you're not simply up to another one of your games..." He paused, his tone indicating he thought she was guilty of the latter. "We do not currently have any job openings."

"That's not what your publicist claims, and it's certainly not what you have posted on your website." She dug through her memory to resurrect a segment of the Genesis creed. "Where innovation and vision collide. Where the world's most introspective minds are ever welcome—"

"Believe me, Ms. Maddox, I am familiar with our corporate creed. There is no need to repeat it. Especially since I have already made my decision concerning your employment."

Fear sliced through her. They were only five

minutes into her interview, and he was shutting her down. "Mr. Calcagni, I—"

He stopped her with an upraised hand. "You may start your two-week trial in the morning. Eight o'clock sharp."

He was actually offering her a job? Or, in this case, a ticket to the next round? According to her inner points tally, she hadn't yet accumulated enough to win. It didn't feel like a victory, either. She had either failed to read some of his cues, or he was better at hiding them than anyone else she'd ever encountered. She no longer had any idea where they stood with each other in their banter of words, who was winning and who was losing. It made her insides weaken to the consistency of jelly.

"Since we have no vacancies in the vice presidency category," he infused an ocean-sized dose of sarcasm into his words, "you'll be serving as my personal assistant. Like every other position on our payroll, it amounts to long hours, hard work, and no coddling. You're under no obligation to accept my offer, of course."

"I accept." She couldn't contain her smile this time. She didn't understand his game, but she'd achieved what she'd come for. Employment. No matter how humble the position. Sometimes it was best not to overthink things. "Thank you, Mr. Calcagni."

There was no answering warmth in him. "You won't be thanking me tomorrow."

"A risk I will gladly take." She rose to seal her commitment with a handshake and immediately realized her mistake.

Standing brought her nearly flush with her new boss. Close enough to catch a whiff of his aftershave — a woodsy musk with a hint of cobra slithering her way. Every organ in her body suffered a tremor beneath the full blast of his scrutiny.

When his long fingers closed over hers, her insides radiated with the same intrinsic awareness of him she'd experienced nine years ago — the day they first met.

It was a complication she hadn't counted on.

I hope you enjoyed this excerpt from
Her Billionaire Boss
Available in eBook and paperback on Amazon + FREE in Kindle Unlimited!

Complete series — read them all!
Her Billionaire Boss
Her Billionaire Bodyguard
Her Billionaire Secret Admirer
Her Billionaire Best Friend
Her Billionaire Geek

Her Billionaire Double Date
Black Tie Billionaires Box Set #1 (Books 1-3)
Black Tie Billionaires Box Set #2 (Books 4-6)

Much love,
Jo

ALSO BY JO GRAFFORD

For the most up-to-date printable list of my books:

Click here

or go to:

https://www.JoGrafford.com/books

For the most up-to-date printable list of books by Jo Grafford, writing as Jovie Grace (*sweet historical romance*):

Click here

or go to:

https://www.jografford.com/joviegracebooks

ABOUT JO

Jo is an Amazon bestselling author of sweet romance stories about faith, hope, love, and family drama with a few Texas-sized detours into humor. She also writes sweet historical romance as Jovie Grace.

1.) Follow on Amazon!
amazon.com/author/jografford

2.) Join Cuppa Jo Readers!
https://www.facebook.com/groups/CuppaJoReaders

3.) Follow on Bookbub!
https://www.bookbub.com/authors/jo-grafford

4.) Follow on Instagram!
https://www.instagram.com/jografford/

5.) Follow on YouTube
https://www.youtube.com/channel/UC3R1at97Qso6BXiBIxCjQ5w

amazon.com/authors/jo-grafford
bookbub.com/authors/jo-grafford
facebook.com/jografford
instagram.com/jografford